Ghost Stories
from the
American
Southwest

Ghost Stories
from the
American
Southwest

Collected and edited by

Richard Alan Young and
Judy Dockrey Young

August House Publishers
LITTLE ROCK

Printed in the United States of America

10 9 8 7 6 5 4 3 2 1   HB
10 9 8 7 6 5 4   PB

LIBRARY OF CONGRESS CATALOGING-IN-PUBLICATION DATA
Ghost stories from the American Southwest / collected and edited by
Richard Alan Young and Judy Dockrey Young.
p.   cm.
Includes index.
ISBN 0-87483-125-3 (hc)
ISBN 0-87483-174-1 (pbk)
1. Tales—Southwest, New. 2. Tales—Southern States.
3. Ghosts—Southwest, New. 4. Ghosts—Southern States. 5. Ghost stories,
American—Southwest, New. 6. Ghost stories, American—Southern States.
I. Young, Richard, 1946- . II. Young, Judy Dockrey, 1949-
GR108.G47   1991
813'.0873308979—dc20   91-10297

Executive: Ted Parkhurst
Project editor: Judith Faust
Design director: Ted Parkhurst
Cover design: Wendell E. Hall
Typography: Spectrum Graphics

AUGUST HOUSE, INC.   PUBLISHERS   LITTLE ROCK

In memoriam
Lewin Hayden Dockrey
January 22, 1920–May 11, 1989
For his love of life and the stories he told

Preface and Acknowledgments

"The preservation and presentation of American heritage through crafts" is one of the objectives of Silver Dollar City, a theme park and crafts village in Branson, Missouri. One aspect of American heritage and one art form (or craft, depending upon your judgment) preserved there is storytelling. The Ozark Mountains, near whose geographic center Silver Dollar City is located, are rich in oral tradition, and the local residents share their stories with visitors from all of the United States and many foreign countries.

We two—Richard Alan Young, a native Texan, and Judy Dockrey Young, an Oklahoma native—have worked at Silver Dollar City as storytellers since 1979 and are the collectors and editors of this anthology of narratives. Many of the stories come from our states of origin; others come from our current homes in Harrison, Arkansas, and Stoneridge, Missouri (a suburb, if you like, of Kimberling City). Still others have been collected during travels to Louisiana, Kansas, Colorado, New Mexico, Arizona, and California, as long ago as 1952 and as recently as 1990. Another source of stories has been the continuous stream of visitors to Silver Dollar City—more than five million of them—since we began storytelling there.

From the "oldest" stories of our childhoods to the most recent acquisitions collected from others in their home states, this anthology represents a broad sample of ghost stories and other supernatural narratives native to, or told in, the American Southwest. Such scary stories are the most popular and most requested stories we know and tell, and it is our pleasure to present them to you.

We wish to express our thanks to all the storytellers and informants who contributed tales for this anthology, whether they did so with recognition, without recognition, or even (at their own request) anonymously. We especially thank those guests of Silver Dollar City who shared stories with us before we ever thought about putting them into an anthology.

Our special thanks go to Teresa Pijoan de Van Etten, New Mexico storyteller and petroglyph expert, who gave us many stories and many story leads; Kathy Costa and the Library Storytellers Guild at Oliver LaFarge Branch of the Santa Fe Public Library; Jim Moeskau, entertainment manager at Silver Dollar City, Missouri; Dr. Gloria A. Young of the University of Arkansas Museum in Fayetteville; Margaret A.E. Miller, resident storyteller at King's Mountain State Park (as of this writing); Shelley Harshbarger, storyteller, of Tallahassee, Florida; and Texas folklorists George D. and Peggy Hendricks of Denton, Texas.

We are grateful for research assistance to Mary Roberts Bishop, Janet Watkins, Lucille Pratt, Bill and Kathy Drake of Sherman Texas, Tilman and Kathryn Cavert of San Antonio, Texas, and Fern Peterson Dockrey of Wagoner, Oklahoma.

We also wish to express our gratitude to Bob Coody and the staff of the Special Collections Library at Northern Arizona University, Dottie House and the library of the Museum of Northern Arizona, Louise Merkel and the staff of the Flagstaff–Coconino County Public Library, and Keith and Kathy Cunningham and the staff of *Southwest Folklore,* all of whom are in Flagstaff, Arizona.

Contents

Haunted Houses 67

Other Haunted Places 87

Introduction

This collection of ghost stories and supernatural narratives is a representative sampling of the broad spectrum of such oral folk literature from the American Southwest. It is not definitive or all-inclusive; it is only a taste of a rich oral tradition that spans centuries of human habitation in the Southwest, from the preliterate societies of native Americans through the illiterate and literate explorers, colonists, and settlers, to the current oral tradition that persists alongside literature both printed and electronically transmitted. The modern Southwesterner will read the latest novel, watch the newest episode of his favorite television program, and then sit around a crackling campfire with fellow hunters or campers or co-workers, listening to and spinning yarns for entertainment and the enrichment of the human experience.

Folklorists document details about the teller as carefully as they document details of the story; the question of whether the teller believes the story to be true is important to a folklorist's scientific interpretation of the meaning and purpose of the story. To storyholders and storytellers, such a question is unimportant to the quality and enduring nature of the story and potentially insulting to the informant or source. For example, many Southwesterners are deeply religious, and the narratives they tell are often part of their belief system. For a storylistener or collector to ask about the personal beliefs of a storyteller with respect to a given story would not be a natural part of the storyholder's task. For this reason, the sources of the stories in this collection are noted in order to give credit to sources and informants, and not solely to illuminate the reader's understanding of the story.

Psychologists and academic folklorists try to explain why human beings tell stories and why they tell stories about the supernatural. As to the question of why people are drawn to and tell stories, storyholders only accept that *it is so,* and thus that it is our task to listen attentively and hold the stories for telling to future generations and broader audiences. This is the task we have undertaken in editing this collection. As to the question of why people listen to, retell, and seem to benefit from the telling of supernatural narratives, storyholders only acknowledge that such stories are the most popular and most often requested narrative type among storylisteners. Having accepted without trying to explain these psychosocial phenomena, we have assembled this collection for a new generation and a broader audience of listeners and readers.

The issue of the religious beliefs of the Southwesterner as they relate to ghost stories is worth further consideration. The editors offer the following observations:

❖ Traditional Christians often tell supernatural stories that are clearly outside the dogma of the Christian church (e.g., narratives about ghosts existing in post-Biblical times, about Satan manifesting himself as a physical being who seems easy to outwit, about God manifesting Himself to humble people, offering them worldly wealth instead of spiritual benefit, and so forth). They are often sensitive about the relationship of such stories to their stated religious beliefs, and many have presented their stories anonymously to us.

❖ Evangelical or charismatic Christians often refuse to listen to or retell supernatural narratives because they seem so outside the stated dogma of their churches. (One may tell the stories of Balaam's talking ass or of the Witch of Endor raising the ghost of Saul or of other Old Testament events, but not the story of a ghostly figure seen in a supposedly haunted house nearby.) In those rare instances when such a believer does relate a non-Biblical supernatural narrative to us, he or she may also do it anonymously. One such person, asked casually about ghost stories, replied, "Stay away from the occult! Stories like that are the work of the Devil!"

❖ Some traditional Christians simply do not tell supernatural narratives. One commented, "We talked about ghosts every day, but it was always the Father, the Son, and the Holy Ghost." Others clearly distinguish between Scriptural truth and fiction for amusement, permitting the latter as long as the narrative is not accepted as fact. These Christians most often tell "ghost jokes" and non-personal, third-person narratives.

❖ Traditional Christians who accept the possibility of modern-day miracles and manifestations often tell supernatural narratives about the works of the Holy Spirit, fully believing the events of the narratives, in the same way "superstitious" people tell ghost stories and accept them as the truth. We have collected some of these.

❖ Traditional practitioners of native American religions tell sacred stories that are part of their belief systems and will often only relate such stories if they are accepted anonymously. Sometimes they will pass them on only when certain small changes have been made during the telling to remove the spiritual power from the stories without altering their message content.

Understanding the deep religious feelings many Southwesterners have is just one aspect of what makes the supernatural narratives of the American Southwest so fascinating and often difficult to collect. Another source of fascination and difficulty is the great variety in interpretation of what constitutes a "ghost story" or supernatural narrative.

Southwesterners may regard as ghost stories or supernatural narratives…

…stories about the works of the Holy Ghost

…stories about spirits or beings in the Ancient Times of native American belief systems

…stories about witches and witchcraft, especially among Hispanic people and among the Navajo

…stories about preternatural beings

…stories about unexplained natural events

…more traditional stories about ghosts as the spirits of deceased persons who have either never left this earth or have returned to it for some reason.

This wide variety of supernatural themes makes the Southwestern narratives much more varied than their Southeastern counterparts, where English, Scottish, Irish, and German ethnic groups share a common interpretation of what constitutes a ghost story.

Another issue that arises in a collection such as this is the definition of the American Southwest. For us, the Southwest is the area west of the Mississippi River and south of the Santa Fe Trail. This vast area encompasses Missouri from the trail-head at St. Louis across to Independence and southward; all of Arkansas, Louisiana, Texas, and Oklahoma; those parts of Kansas south of the Arkansas River; Colorado along and south of the Arkansas River; and all of New Mexico and Arizona. The southern portions of Utah, Nevada, and California are partly Southwestern in culture and partly Great Northwestern. Our collection touches them only briefly. (There is ample material from these states for other anthologies of narratives from the Great Northwest—the Pacific Northwest, the Rocky Mountain States, and the western Great Plains—or even just from California itself.)

No attempt has been made to collect from traditional narratives state-by-state or by ethnic groups; rather, these stories came to us from interested people living in the areas listed. The stories are arranged by general theme rather than by region or ethnicity, but there is an index of stories by state of origin.

The method of collection was simple: storytellers generally share stories, each teller present offering his or her narratives around a fireplace or some other appropriate storytelling setting.

The stories come in many forms:

...complete stories with well-developed plot lines and character delineation, rising action that culminates in a climax, and all the aspects of a well-told story

...short, almost summarized, versions of what was previously heard by the teller as a complete story

...fragments of a story, with many lacunae ("holes" where elements have obviously been lost or forgotten) and often no ending

...sometimes just a single item or element, such as the name of a story, of a character, or of a place associated with the supernatural.

When stories come to us incomplete, we do not try to fill in the missing portions ourselves; we wait patiently until another teller gives us another version with some of the missing portions included. Eventually the story is filled in and becomes complete, ready for telling. When one version has an "extra element" that is missing from all the other versions we have heard, and does not seem to supply a lacuna, we often choose to omit that extra element from the finished story.

Our purpose in this collection is not the preservation of numerous variants verbatim, but the preservation and presentation of the story in its complete, if generalized, form. This "retelling form" of the narrative represents the way it is told in its most complete version by the majority of those who tell it. This is not the folklorist's method of preserving a single variant ("frozen in time and space"), but it represents the storyteller's method of preservation with minimal alteration by the collectors/tellers. The storyteller himself or herself is one link in the human chain that transmits the story over time, and is one of the "folks" in the unbroken chain of folklore; the same is true for the story collector or storyholder. The folklorist, on the other hand, is likely to be more emotionally detached from the story and is a scientist and scholar outside the actual folklore chain, looking in as an observer.

Ghost stories range from the disdainfully-told fragment or summary of a legend to gripping personal narratives that bring a tear to the eye of the teller. As storytellers and storyholders, we listen without judging, without trying to decide if the story is true or not. It is not the truth that matters, it is the story—and there is a general truth even in stories that are not specifically true. Here are examples of the extremes of personal emotional involvement with a narrative:

> They say that years ago at Fort Sill [an Army outpost now in the state of Oklahoma], you could see two ghosts quarrel in one of the barracks buildings. Two cavalry soldiers were in love with the same girl. They died in the Indian Wars, and their ghosts keep coming back to see their girlfriend. This is an old story.[1]

I saw her! *La LLorona!* I was nine years old, and it was late in the day on a Saturday, late in the fall, around Hallowe'en. Me and my friend—another nine-year-old—and two eleven-year-olds and a thirteen-year-old, we decided we were going to go over to the schoolground and play on the merry-go-round, in my hometown of Las Vegas [New Mexico]. *La LLorona,* you know, she was the one who killed her children after World War I. I saw her.

You see, to get to the school from my house over near the railroad tracks and Gallinas [River], we went down the tracks where it's real dark. We were at some abandoned sheds, along the tracks, and I picked up some rocks and was throwing them to see if I could get one to go in the holes in the wall of the shed.

I was just getting to the last shed, and I saw this mattress folded over lying beside the last shed, and on it this white, white shape. I took a rock and I threw it. It hit the white form, and it… started to come up off the mattress. I crouched down and put my hands up over my head, and this form, it just came up off of the mattress and it started floating at me and wailing that terrible wail…"*Ni-i-i-ño-o-o…ni-i-i-ño-o-o…* [My son, my son]."

The other kids ran away. Me, I was so scared I couldn't run.

I crouched down with my arms over my head, and when I looked up, she went over my head, and she went over the railroad tracks, and she went over to the river, and she disappeared.

I got up and I ran. I ran so fast that I caught up to those older boys, and we all looked at each other and we knew, we knew. We had seen *la LLorona!*[2]

In the first narrative, the teller merely summarizes the events of a story he has heard, or heard of. He does not tell the story himself (nor, as the folklorist would point out, does he seem to believe the story). In the second example, collected by Betsy McWilliams, a Hispanic folklorist, the young Hispano teller is deeply involved in this very personal narrative which, according to the collector, was related with strong emotional context.

One type of story that shows the extremes of personal involvement is the "ghost-light story." There is no scary story type more beloved. Almost everyone in the Southwest has heard at least one ghost-light story, and there are several very famous lights or sets of lights in the region: The Marfa Lights in Texas, the Hornet Light in Missouri, and others. Visiting these lights is a favorite pastime, especially for young adults. Serious studies and frivolous legends have yet to explain the phenomena, even though such diverse groups as the U. S. Army Corps of Engineers, the film crew of television's "Unsolved Mysteries," and scientists from local colleges and universities have tried. When we asked for "spooklight" stories, we got many answers, such as:

> The spooklight at Hornet [Missouri, near Joplin] has been explained by a scientist as a phenomenon of lights on the Will Rogers Turnpike across the [state] line in Oklahoma. But the light was seen long before that road was ever put in, or even before there were automobiles with electric lights.[3]

Most spooklight stories are explanations of why the light exists or are chilling personal accounts of going (often on a dare) to the site of the ghostly glow. We have included both kinds of narratives in this collection. Here are further examples:

> This story is called "Bailey's Lantern." Out on Bailey's Prairie [in Texas] there is a ghost-light that can be seen on the darkest nights. It has been seen for over a hundred years. A settler named Bailey, who arrived before Stephen F. Austin's band, quarrelled with Austin over his squatter's rights [which Austin would have claimed violated the terms of Austin's land grant from Mexico]. Bailey, a hard drinker, swore "never to leave his land, dead or alive."
> As he lay dying, years later, he asked to be buried standing up, holding a bottle of good whiskey, facing west, since he'd been going west all his life anyway. Some relatives saw his ghost as early as the 1830s; now there's only his light, a lantern, seen near the [presumed] site of his unmarked grave.[4]

Next, an example of the somewhat rare "second person narrative," in which the teller uses the American English tendency to replace the pronoun *one* with the pronoun *you,* and in which a feeling of immediacy is created for the listener:

> You know the Rio Grande [River] along at Laredo [Texas]? You can see a ghost-light there! The Mexican town of Dolores is there, too. They used to mine silver there, and if you go there along by the river at night, you can see a lantern moving along the trail in the darkness. You can't see who's holding it, just the lantern. You might see just a hand with no body attached, holding the lantern. It's a miner who was killed in a cave-in and he lost his hand. You can see him still looking for his silver.[5]

One final example of a very personal ghost-light narrative:

> My father is a riverboat man, and he calls two very different things by the name *feu follé* [also spelled *feu follet* in some books]. As you go down the river you can see images in the swamp gas that escapes out of holes or bubbles; sometimes it would shoot up like a jet, and sometimes it would look like fire. Most often it looks like fire: *feu follé.*
>
> Also, when it is stormy and lightning is dancing on the wire fence, like what some people call St. Elmo's Fire, he also calls that *feu follé.* [The informant pronounces the phenomenon as if it were written *fifollé* in French.][6]

From the folklorist's point of view, the stories we have collected are one small part of folklore. "Folklore" is often defined as material that is transmitted orally, is usually traditional and formulaic (unless it is a very personal experience being passed on), changes with time and retelling thereby creating variants (changing with the style of the teller and the signs of the times; e.g. a traveller on horseback becomes a driver of a car, etc.), is often anonymous (except for personal experiences), and often has no title (unless the teller thinks of the story as being traditional and easily identifiable by the title).

Storytellers are often described as "active bearers of folklore" who actively retell and keep alive their stories. Carl W. von Sydow, who conceived of this classification, called "passive bearers of folklore" those who only know summaries or have dim recollections that they can repeat if asked to, but who are not likely to tell the stories or remember them without being asked. Here are examples:

In Valencia County [New Mexico] three dead men who were hanged as outlaws come back and haunt the place of their death. Some people call it *El árbol de la horca.*[7]

Sometimes the narratives are disconnected thoughts that reflect a more complex folk belief or that refer in fragmentary form to a longer story, heard in childhood and now forgotten:

You know, if a place is haunted you can put a thin layer of ash on something—a table or something—and leave a feather. Then the spirits will write in the ash what it is they want. And you can give them what they want, and they will go away. They have to use a feather because it is light, and they are not very strong, you know. [Collected in southern New Mexico.][8]

Sometimes the narratives are told in story form, but only as a summary, not as an "adventure tale":

A story about a hairy man is told by folks east of here [Waco, Texas]. He lives along Richland Creek and the Trinity River. He hasn't been seen recently, maybe in the 40s, but he has a huge head and—this is the interesting part—his hands and feet are alike, as if he were really a four-footed creature. He's usually seen near the creek or near a well.[9]

Finally, the narratives are sometimes told as real stories, often complete with appropriate gestures and sound effects, as the events are presumed to have happened to a third party or as the teller asserts the events actually happened to him or her. These stories are generally the work of active bearers of folklore who will offer their tales "at the drop of a hat."

The most active bearers of folklore and the most ardent tellers of ghost stories often offer narratives that are actually death beliefs or events associated with death beliefs. In spite of the fact that these are not "stories" in the strict sense, they are folklore, and have sometimes been included in this collection. Here is a lengthy example from a good teller:

> My mother is an L.P.N. and was hired a few years back to sit with [an elderly man] who was dying at home. The old man had lost his mind and was very threatening and abusive to his family, but he was too weak to do anything, and my mother wasn't in any danger. She was sitting with him one day, reading a book while he was asleep, when he rattled and died.
>
> When she was sure that he was really dead, she informed the family and started the long walk to a telephone at a house a mile away to call the ambulance and the coroner.
>
> As she was leaving the house, one of the menfolk was slowly peeling the wallpaper in the room with the dead man and another was outside with a clawhammer pulling off siding. When she got back an hour later, and the ambulance came, the family had taken off the siding, opened a hole in the lath, and peeled back the wallcovering to make an opening two feet tall and as wide as the studs. They made the E.M.T.s pass the body out the hole in the wall rather than letting it be taken out a door or window. When Mother asked why, they said simply, "to keep his ghost away."
>
> As everyone left, they were nailing the siding back in place.[10]

All the sources and informants who told us stories used vivid language imagery to describe the ghosts or supernatural and preternatural beings and events being narrated. The most striking words were those chosen by the tellers to denominate the ghosts or beings themselves. Tellers who were dubious about the objects of their narratives used works like *shape, form, figure,* or just *thing* to name ghostlike phenomena. A few believers in ghosts or psychic phenomena used words like *vision, aura, emanation,* or *materialization.* Others used the terms *shadow, specter, soul,* or the skeptical terms *illusion* or *hallucination.*

The most common terms were *ghost, phantom, spook, phantasm, apparition, spirit, wraith, spectre* (specter) and even *will-o'-the-wisp* (will-o-wisp). The poetic word *shade* and the rather technical term *revenant* have never come up in stories told to us. In the Ozarks, the terms *haint* [haunt] for ghost and *booger* (as a prefix, e.g. booger dog) for preternatural being are very common; these terms are also found (less frequently) anywhere the "mountain folks" or "hillbillies" settled in the late 1800s.

A few ethnic groups have unique words in their native languages that come into English stories (e.g., the Irish *banshee*), or names for specific beings that are universally accepted (e.g., *la LLorona*), but for the most part the stories we have heard, retold, or collected used common but expressive English vocabulary. (One exception is the very few Native American Indian stories in which the informants used indigenous language names that we have phonetically rendered without tonal or diacritical markings.) Although some Southwestern states have passed legislation in recent years making English the "official language" of that state (e.g. Arkansas, California), it is common usage that makes English the preferred language (even as a *lingua franca*) of the Southwest. The Vietnamese grocer tells the Navajo customer what his Hispanic neighbor told him about a haunted place; the story is in English.

Each ethnic and linguistic group has its own rich heritage of oral traditions in its native tongue, and each such heritage richly deserves study and preservation in that tongue. We think this collection of narratives, a general sampling of the American Southwest with all its cultural diversity, is equally rich in the unique dialect we call American English.

NOTES

[1] Collected from an unidentified Oklahoma man, a white male in his thirties, in 1988.

[2] "I Saw Her!" collected by Hispanic folklorist Betsy McWilliams in September, 1990, at Cochiti Lake, New Mexico, from "Miguel," a young hispano in his twenties.

[3] Collected from Bill Frenchman in October, 1989. An Oklahoma resident, Mr. Frenchman has travelled and observed the ghost-light phenomenon in several Southwestern states.

[4] "Bailey's Lantern," provided by a patron of the library in San Antonio, Texas, in November, 1989. A white male in his fifties, he told the story enthusiastically but did not seem to believe the events of the story.

[5] Collected from a stall-keeper at the Mercado in Nuevo Laredo, Mexico, across from Laredo, Texas, in the 1970s. The Hispanic male in his forties told the story in English and appeared to accept the events as the truth. He used the English "you" to mean "one" as native English-speakers do.

[6] Collected from Louis Darby of Opelousas, Louisiana, former Louisiana state fiddle champion, in August, 1989.

[7] "El árbol de la horca," collected from a young Hispanic male in his twenties, from southern New Mexico, in late summer, 1988.

[8] Collected from a young Hispanic male waiter in a restaurant in Mesilla, New Mexico, in January, 1987. The young man, in his twenties, seemed to believe the data to be true.

[9] "The East Texas Hairy Man," provided by a librarian in Waco, Texas, who declined to be identified, in November, 1989. *Compare this summary with the events in story number 104.*

[10] Collected from a teen-aged white male living in Boone County, Arkansas, in 1972. The events took place in Newton County, Arkansas, in about 1969. To avoid any unethical implications of patient confidentiality, names and some details have been deleted.

There always exists the possibility that stories told orally to the editors of this collection may have passed through the print medium (i.e., the stories are told orally, written down by a collector, and read by someone who then tells them orally to another collector). It should be noted that "Bailey's Lantern" (note 4) is also recorded in Catherine Munson Foster's *Ghosts Along the Brazos* (Texian Press, Waco, Texas, 1977), and the Dolores-Light story (note 5) resembles a series of statements in Henry Yelvington's *Ghost Lore* (The Naylor Company, San Antonio, Texas, 1936). Both stories, however, are well known in their respective areas and may have reached our informants purely through the oral tradition.

Notes on the text

The spelling of certain American Indian names and words is often phonetic rather than the official spelling used in each language, especially if the official spelling involves tonal or diacritical markings. The editors apologize for any inconsistencies or errors with respect to the American Indian languages, in which we are not conversant.

The spelling of words in Spanish follows the forms given to us by native speakers or the correct forms for the dialect of Spanish most familiar to the editors. The capitalization of the Spanish letter *ll*, as in *la LLorona,* follows the historic, though antique, pattern for the American Southwest and conforms to the spelling the editors learned from parents and collateral relatives who spoke the language. We use it everywhere except in story 132, where we preserve the spelling of the title in the orginal printed version.

The spelling of the name Jean Laffite (instead of *Lafitte*) is based on the fact that Laffite himself is known to have signed his name with that spelling.

Parentheses in the introduction and the text of the narratives indicate normally parenthetical material; brackets represent insertions, deletions, or explanations by the editors. In all cases of deletion, personal names or personal information was left out at the specific request of the source or informant.

Titles have been given to the narratives to make the book easier to browse. In most instances, they are simply descriptive phrases chosen by the editors to help keep track of separate stories. Where the title is one used by informants or customarily attached to a story, it will be indicated in the notes, all of which are gathered in the back of the book.

Ghost Jokes

1 The Pawpaw Lie

It was autumn, and two boys had been out stealing pawpaws from under a neighbor's tree. Their families didn't have good pawpaw trees, and the fruit was just ripe, so they waited until the fellow with the good tree was out milking, and they crept into his yard and stole a whole bagful. With two boys and only one sack, they had to divide up the goods. They figured that since it was sundown, the least likely place for them to be disturbed was the graveyard.

So they went to the graveyard, and hid behind a big, tall head marker just inside the rock wall, and started dividing up the pawpaws, saying, "You take this one, I'll take that one."

While they were counting, this big old cornfed country boy came swinging along the road whistling to himself. He stopped just as he got alongside the boys on the back of the wall. He heard them real clearly saying, "You take this one, I'll take that one."

It scared that country boy to death. He took off running all the way to the house.

When he got to the porch, he hollered, "Pop! Pop! I heard them! It was the Lord and the Devil out in the graveyard dividing up the souls!"

By the time he got inside the house, his father said, "Son, you've been in the liquor again, haven't you?"

"No, Pop, really!" said the boy, jumping up and down with excitement. "I heard them dividing up the souls, going 'You take this one, I'll take that one!' Really I did!"

"Son," said the old man, "if you heard that, I want to hear it, too."

"Well, come on, let's go!" said the boy, starting out the door.

"Son," said the old man, "you know I ain't stirred a step with the rheumatism these ten solid years. You'll have to carry me. That's what I raised you big old boys for. Pick me up and carry me down there."

So the great big boy grabbed the skinny old man and set him on his shoulders, and off they went to the graveyard. As they got closer and closer the boy went slower and slower, until he was creeping up on the graveyard wall, old man and all. Those two boys were still there, but they were through dividing up the good pawpaws, and were down to the last two.

Just as the country boy and the old man got to the wall and leaned over to listen, one of the thieves said, "There's not but these two left. You take that big fat one and I'll take the old shriveled-up one."

That was it! The country boy reared back and threw his old grey-haired father off and lit out running toward the house. And his pop, who hadn't stirred a step with the rheumatism for ten solid years, beat the boy home by a full minute!

2 *You Can't Get Out*

A young man was walking through the graveyard one night, and he fell into a fresh-dug hole left open for a funeral the next day. He wasn't hurt, and he tried and tried to get out. No matter how he scrambled and jumped, the hole was just too deep. He finally settled down to spend a cold night in the ground until the mortician would come in the morning.

A few hours later, a drunk came walking through the graveyard, whistling loudly. Sure enough, he fell in, too.

The young man sat in the corner watching the drunk jumping and scrambling, trying to get out.

Finally, to be helpful, the young man said to the drunk, "You know, you can't get out."

But, you know, he did!

3 *I Can't Get In*

My granddaddy grew up in Newton County [Arkansas]. He's dead now, but when I was a boy he told me that this happened to him. He and a friend had been to a dance and had got drunk on moonshine. It was real strong stuff, and both boys were sick and staggering. They lived side-by-side and were walking each other home, trying to stay standing-up on the road.

They came to the graveyard and knew they could shortcut through it. They got about halfway through, and the other boy got sick and sat down on a grave to let his head stop spinning. Granddaddy went on. About five minutes later, the other boy ran past Granddaddy like he was standing still.

Granddaddy ran crazily, trying to keep up, and when he got to the other boy's front porch, there he was, shaking like a leaf and stone-cold sober.

"What happened?" asked Granddaddy.

"I was sitting on that grave," said the other boy, "and somebody starting poking me on the shoulder. I looked up. It was a skeleton standing beside me, poking me on the shoulder and saying, 'I can't get in. You're in my way! I can't get in!' "

Granddaddy swore it was the truth.

4 *The Haunted Car*

Once there was a circuit preacher in north Texas who was preaching in a small town on a Sunday that fell on Hallowe'en. After the service was over in the old wooden church house, the preacherman stayed to let the fire die out before he locked up for the month and walked to the farmhouse where he was staying with members of the congregation. He scattered the coals and covered them with ash, turned the damper down, and shuttered the windows. The wind was blowing cold when he locked the door and started down the dirt road toward the farmplace.

He had to walk over three hills and down through two gullies to get where he was going, and on the middle hill sat the old graveyard. As he walked, he pulled his scarf up and his hat down to turn the wind. Soon he heard something on the road behind him. He stepped aside and looked back in the darkness, but a grove of live-oak trees on the eastern horizon kept him from seeing the outline of whatever was behind him.

He turned back around and kept on walking. A minute or two later, he heard something behind him again, getting closer. There weren't any hoofbeats, so it wasn't a horse; there weren't any tracechains jingling, so it wasn't a wagon; there wasn't any motor noise, so it wasn't a tractor or an automobile. He stopped again to listen, but the sound had stopped. He kept on walking, up the slope toward the graveyard.

The preacherman heard the sound again, and it was so close behind him that it made the hair on the back of his neck stand up. He turned around, and saw a huge, black shape coming silently at him. He stepped aside, and the shape pulled alongside of him. It was an automobile, but without its lights lit.

"Well," thought the preacherman, "this is some deacon of the church who's taken some sister home and is stopping to offer me a ride." He stepped over, opened the side door, and got into the back seat. He leaned forward to thank whoever was driving, but he found he was alone in the vehicle.

And the automobile began to move...silently...toward the graveyard!

The preacher sat very still and waited until the vehicle rolled to a stop—right in front of the iron gate to the burying ground.

"Well," thought the preacher, "I guess this is where I'm supposed to get out." He stepped out of the automobile, shut the door quietly, and walked quickly away from the ghostly vehicle. Suddenly, he heard something breathing heavily, like a huge animal, just on the other side of a tall marble monument.

Very slowly, the preacherman walked around the marble stone and saw...one of the deacons of the church, leaning on the marble and breathing loud and hard.

"Don't go near that automobile!" said the preacher. "There's something wrong with it!"

"I know that, Brother John," said the deacon. "I've been pushing the damn thing for a mile!"

5 A Ghost Story for Folklorists

Once, on a dare, a young man H1416. He fell asleep, and at midnight the E273 and suddenly E279.2. The young man jumped up and saw E530.1 all around him and heard E401! Up from behind a huge tombstone D1641.13 and it F1083.0.1 toward him.

He began to run, and it chased him as F99O!

He ran all around the graveyard and finally took a cough drop and stopped the D1641.13.

Translation

Once, on a dare to prove his bravery, a young man spent the night in a graveyard. He fell asleep, and at midnight the ghosts of the dead woke up and started talking to each other. That woke the young man. He jumped up and saw the ghosts glowing and talking to each other, and just then a coffin floated up out of an open grave and came toward the young man.

He ran and ran, and the coffin chased him.

He ran all around the graveyard and finally took a cough drop and stopped the coughin'.

6 Scary Song

There was an old woman,
She was just skin and bones,
Oh, oh, oh-oo!
There was an old woman,
She was just skin and bones,
Oh, oh, oh-oo!
Well, she looked up and she looked down,
She spied a corpse upon the ground,
Oh, oh, oh-oo!
She went to the parson and she said,
Will I look so when I am dead?

Oh, oh, oh-oo?
And the parson said
[shouted] *Yes!*

❖ Editors' note: The editors have heard many other "ghost jokes"
through the years, but these six are the most typical and the best
examples of this popular Southwestern genre. We have heard
dozens of variants on each, from countless tellers. Many other
such narratives base their humor on racial or ethnic insults, or are
scatological, or lack good narrative form, and have been omitted.
While such narratives have value to a folklorist, a storyholder or
storyteller might choose not to pass them along.

Urban Legends

7 Last Kiss

Late one night, years ago, a teen-age boy was driving home on a Saturday night, on a rainy road in the country. Just as he rounded a long curve, the headlights lit up a teen-age girl standing by the highway. She was wearing a white party dress, but she was all wet from the rain. He knew at once what must have happened: her date had dumped her after a quarrel. He felt so sorry for her that he skidded to a stop before she even had a chance to hail him.

He leaned over and opened the door for her, and she got in.

"Would you take me home?" she asked. "I just live a mile down the road."

He noticed for the first time how really pretty she was. He almost couldn't speak, she was so pretty. He mumbled something and she smiled. He quickly took off his letter jacket, and she leaned forward in the seat so he could drape it over her shoulders to keep her warm. It was too crowded in the car for her to get her arms into the sleeves.

The boy put the car in gear, and they were at the two-story house by the graveyard before he could even think of anything to say.

"This is my house," she said.

He stopped the car and got out and went around to open the door for her. He walked her up onto the porch of the dark house, and before he could think how to ask if he could see her again, she kissed him. He was so surprised that she opened the screen door, opened the front door, and was gone into the darkness before he could speak. Then he realized that she still had on his jacket.

It was a perfect excuse to see her again. He could come back the next day after church and ask for his jacket.

Sunday afternoon, he was back at the house and knocked on the door. A haggard woman came to the door.

He asked if he could see her daughter.

"My daughter died one year ago last night," said the woman sadly. "She was killed in a car wreck at the big curve down the road, there."

He told her that wasn't possible, that he had given her a ride home the night before.

"If you don't believe me," she replied, "go look in the cemetery, there. Her tombstone is in the third row."

The boy walked slowly into the graveyard. In the third row of headstones, he found the one he was looking for.

There was his letter jacket, draped over the rounded grave marker, just like it had hung around her shoulders on Saturday night.

8 *Laffite's Hook-Arm*

There's this cemetery in the outskirts of New Orleans where the ghost of Jean Laffite is seen walking on moonless nights. He wears a pirate hat and has a hook instead of his left hand.

One night, two kids were going parking on the old road by the cemetery, where no one would bother them. While they were parked, the girl thought she heard something outside in the graveyard. To get her to snuggle close to him, the boy told her the story of Laffite's ghost.

The trick backfired, though, and the girl got so scared that she demanded he take her home. He had just about decided she must not like him. To be polite, he started up the car, and just as they pulled onto the road, there was a loud thud on her side of the car. The girl screamed, and the boy stomped on the gas and spun out down the road.

Back at the girl's house, the boy got out and went around to open her door. He just stood there, staring down at the door. At first the girl couldn't figure out what was wrong. Then she realized the door was locked, and he must be waiting for her to unlock it. But even when she unlocked the door, he just stood there staring.

The girl rolled her window down, and looked out at the door handle. Hanging from the handle was an old brass hook, with a stream of dried blood trailing off the door!

9 The Baby's Milk Bottles

They tell a story about a store owner in the Santa Clara Valley during the Great Depression. One rainy day, a woman in a print cotton dress, drenched by a sudden rainstorm, came into the store with two empty returnable milk bottles. She set them on the counter without a word, folded her arms, and looked down. The store owner assumed she wanted two more bottles. He got them from the cooler and set them in front of her, putting the empties underneath the counter. He told her the price was ten cents.

She took the fresh milk without speaking, and left without paying. The store owner just sighed; she probably didn't have any money anyway.

The next day she came back, and put the empties on the counter. She stepped back, folded her arms, and stared straight ahead. After a moment, the owner put the empties away and gave her two more fresh bottles out of the cooler. She left without paying, almost running out the door.

The third day, she came back with the empties. The store owner felt so sorry for the skinny, bedraggled woman that he took her empties and gave her fresh milk. But this time he followed a few yards behind her when she went quickly out the door. Maybe he could find the migrant camp where she was staying and give someone in her family a job around the store.

Instead of going to the migrant camps by the road, the woman went to the graveyard by the river. She disappeared behind a stone marker just as it began to rain again. The owner stood there for a few minutes, getting wet, and then he decided to leave. Just as he turned to go, he heard a baby crying in the distance. He looked all around the graveyard for a tent or migrant camp. Then he realized the muffled cries were coming from under his feet.

From inside a shallow grave!

The man ran back to the store and called everyone he knew that had a phone. In a few minutes trucks began to descend on the graveyard. Men with shovels had the grave open in a matter of moments. Inside was the woman in the cotton dress. She was dead, and had been for days. In her arms was the baby who'd been buried with her—but the baby was alive.

Beside the baby were two bottles of fresh milk.

10   Pair of Pants

An old woman and an old man lived together in a slat house by the river. When the old man died, the woman sold most of his clothing to pay for the funeral. When the funeral director told her the casket's half-lid is opened only from the waist up at funerals, the old woman sold the old man's pants.

After the funeral, the ghost came to her at night. He stood in the door to the bedroom night after night, staring at the old woman. She'd just scream and cover her head with the bedclothes until dawn. Finally she went to the preacher and asked what to do.

"Ask him 'what in the name of the Lord' he wants," said the preacher.

That night the ghost came again.

"What in the name of the Lord do you want?" she asked.

"I'm cold," he said. "I want my pants."

"All right," she said. "I'll go get them."

The ghost went away and never came back. And the old woman didn't go get the pants back, either.

11   Freshman Initiation

Years ago, when I was in junior high school, I was on the track team. The senior high boys made us freshmen spend the night in a haunted house outside of town as a kind of initiation. They'd been doing it for years, and no one thought much about it, except that the kids that had come from the house always said it really was a scary place. We always expected that the seniors would be doing something to try to scare us, anyway, so we were ready for it.

The night started out pretty normal, with the five of us—I come from a small town—in the living room. We didn't have any lights, the seniors didn't allow that, and we'd been told to split up, one to a room, to get some sleep. I took the old living room, Dave got the back room, and so on; John took the lonely upstairs room. Well, we heard pebbles hit the windowpanes from time to time, and ghostly moans came from the barn out back, but by midnight the upperclassmen hadn't done anything really scary, or that we could conclusively blame on them, and it got real quiet and still. I guess we all fell asleep.

I awoke past midnight and could hear John in the room upstairs pacing slowly back and forth in his big heavy work boots that he always wore. I guess it woke everyone up, because the other four of us all got to the foot of the stairs at the same time, looking at each other kind of scared. We called to John and he didn't answer, but the pacing stopped.

The wind was blowing outside, and the old curtains were blowing in at the windows. Slowly, we climbed the stairs to the loft, in the inky darkness. Then, at the top of the stairs, we saw it: it was John, at least it had John's big shoes and John's clothes. We couldn't tell if it had John's face, because it had no head. Then the thing slowly lifted its head from the darkness beside itself, and threw the head right at us!

We ran as fast as we could back down the stairs and scattered out of the way. The head hit the floor. It was a burlap bag full of barn dirt. We ran back up the stairs, realizing we'd been tricked. John must have been in on it with the upperclassmen. They were probably laughing themselves silly somewhere out on the roof. In the loft, we found muddy tracks. The window was open. We ran back downstairs and scattered out to surround the house.

Around back, we found John all right, and we were sure it was John, but he had tried to climb out the back window and slide down to the low part of the roof for a drop to the ground. He must have slipped and slid faster than he planned. The old roof was sheets of tin, and a gable cut across over the kitchen. He must have hit the rusty edge of the gable sliding pretty fast. He was on the ground. His head was lying on the edge of the kitchen gable, staring down at us.

We let out a scream, and Dave turned and ran. While we tried to think of something to do, Bob noticed Dave was nowhere in sight. As we started the long run to town to get the sheriff, we saw Bob standing over the well. There in the light of the rising moon, was Dave, lying in the shallow well where he must have fallen when he ran, with his neck broken.

The upperclassmen denied having John "in" on the trick; it must have been his own idea. At least Dave's funeral could have an open casket. Bob went catatonic and has been lying in a bed in the state hospital ever since. Butch committed suicide the next year.

That just leaves me. But I'm all right, aren't I?

Aren't I?

12 Call from the Grave

One time there was a little girl whose grandfather had just died. She had loved her grandfather very much, and she missed him a great deal. He was buried in the cemetery just a hundred yards from the home. She could see his grave from the living room window.

One night her parents were going out, and the babysitter hadn't come yet. They knew she was very reliable and would probably arrive in just a few minutes, so they kissed the girl goodbye and left for the drive into the city. Hours passed, and the babysitter still had not come; the girl began to be afraid. A storm was brewing outside, and thunder and lightning began to move closer to the house. Suddenly the lights went out just as a flash of lightning struck close to the home. The wind blew and branches fell all around the yard. Alone in the dark, the girl began to cry.

Then the phone rang. Just once. She went to it and answered, hoping it was her parents. She said hello, but no one said anything for a long time. Then a voice said, very softly and very far away, "Don't be afraid, honey. There's nothing to fear. You'll be safe in the house, and the storm will pass over..."

It was her grandfather. She waited a long time, but there was no other sound on the line. Slowly she hung up and sat down on the sofa, smiling.

Her parents drove hurriedly into the driveway, dodging the fallen branches, and rushed up to the door. The girl met them at the door, smiling, in the dark.

They told her that they had tried to call, but the phones were all dead. She told them she had gotten just one call. From her grandfather. The parents just shook their heads and put the girl to bed.

The next day, the family went to the cemetery to clean up around the grave after the storm. Branches were down everywhere; the power lines were down, and the phone lines were hanging off the poles. The phone line from the house was intact up to the first pole, then it fell into the cemetery— where they found it lying with its broken end across the grandfather's grave.

13 *Eleven-Eleven*

There's a mysterious time of day; you only notice it if you have a digital clock. Once you've heard this story, you'll know that it's true. That ghostly time is 11:11. Here's what happened:

It was the big party at the high school. All the kids were having a great time. Nobody noticed that the captain of the football team and his girlfriend, the head cheerleader, had left early to go out and get drunk.

Nobody alive knows how it happened, but their car skidded off the road and hit a tree, killing them both instantly. Back at the dance, it was like everyone had this same feeling all at the same time. They all turned and looked at the digital clock on the desk. It was 11:11, the exact moment the kids had died.

And after that, the teenagers began to know that their dead friends were trying to communicate with them, trying to warn them with the ghostly message. They began to notice the clock when it said 11:11.

And now that you've heard the story, it will happen to you, too. You'll get the ghostly message. You'll start noticing the time, over and over again, for the rest of your life, just as the digital clock reads 11:11.

14 *La LLorona at Waldo*

Now this happened to a friend of mine, and so I know it's true. He was in his pick-up, driving from Cerrillos to I-25, and he was drinking beer and throwing the cans out the window. He was at Waldo [a ghost town], and he saw this girl hitchhiking. It was real late at night, and so he picked her up because she looked like she was lost or had run away from home.

And he was driving on this gravel road, and there's no houses or anything near. And she says to him that he shouldn't drink so much. And he just laughed and threw another empty can out. And when he looked over at her, she was all ugly, and her face was starting to rot like she'd been dead for a long time. And he looked away because she was so ugly, and when he looked back, she was gone.

And it was *la LLorona,* and that's true.

Ghostly Lights

15   Michael and the Ghost Light

On a dark night, in the heat of summer, we left the sawmill where we worked and drove eighty miles to see it: the ghost light at Crossett. Four of us in a convertible with the top down; one of the guys had been there before and knew the way. It was about ten o'clock when we stopped on the gravel road and turned out the lights. The railbed is elevated in that part of the state. The road rose about three feet above the level of the fields to cross the single set of rails.

We sat in the car drinking and talking, waiting for something to happen, daring and double-dog-daring each other to approach the light if it appeared. Somebody retold the legend in the steamy darkness:

A train had rolled to a stop just at this crossing sometime after the turn of the century on a dark, hot night like this one. A brakeman was walking the railbed with a lantern, checking the cars or the couplings. Something, no one knew what, caught his attention between two cars; leaning in at the coupling, he found something wrong.

Trying to fix something, a loose coupling or a dragging chain, he bent closer and closer to the metal mechanism. The locomotive lurched a few inches along the track as steam engines sometimes did, and a heavy ripple of movement surged down the long line of flatcars and boxcars. The brakeman's lantern fell to the railbed.

Looking back past the coal car, the engineer saw the lantern fall. He took his own lantern and ran back, car after car, to where the brakeman's lantern lay. The body was lying across the track. The head was lying under a bloody coupling. Some folks say the body went that night in a boxcar, but the head was left behind, no one having the courage to pick it up. Or maybe the head just wasn't in the boxcar with the body.

Anyway, by night, people still see the light of the lantern moving slowly along the tracks about three feet off the ground. "It's the decapitated brakeman," people say, "still looking for his head!"

The convertible got very quiet after the last retelling of the legend.

An instant later we saw it. A faint, yellowish ball of light about a foot in diameter was floating slowly along the tracks, three feet above the rails, going south to north. It just crept along, not bobbing or weaving, just slow and steady.

Finally, I left the car and walked toward the tracks, not ever taking my eyes off the light, trying to meet it at the intersection on a double-dog-dare. I was sweating, but I wasn't sure why. There wasn't any fear, or any feeling at all, just that light. I got onto the tracks and turned and faced it as it came slowly toward me. When it got within ten feet of me, it just vanished.

I was almost disappointed. After a minute, I turned to walk back to the car. There was the light, north of me on the tracks, moving away. The guys were all wide-eyed as I came up to the car.

"What did it feel like?" they asked.

"What did what feel like?" I said.

"We saw the ghost light pass right through your chest!"

Then, and only then, was I afraid. Really afraid.

16 Dawson Cemetery

The Dawson Cemetery sits alone on a hill, the town it once served long gone. In the silver mining country near Cimarron, New Mexico, Dawson was a boom town, and it went bust just as quickly when a cave-in killed most of the men in town. A second cave-in twenty-five years later ended the town's life. Most of the headstones in the cemetery have one of the two cave-in dates. The town itself was dismantled board by board and carried off by the mining company when the second cave-in made the mine unprofitable.

Some of the rangers from Philmont Ranch would drive out to the cemetery with a guitar and something to drink, and sit around watching the moon and enjoying an evening off. Myself and three other rangers from the [Air Force] Academy, and two civilian rangers, went out one summer night in 1980 and sat around enjoying the high desert view and the old songs.

[One of the rangers present] got uneasy, and wandered back to the car, parked a hundred yards away. Later, another ranger went down to the car to check on the... not exactly scared, just uneasy... friend. Only minutes later, the second fellow came walking quickly back to the grave sites. He grabbed me by the arm and whispered, "We all need to leave here, right now!"

He was dead serious, as serious as a stone, and we all packed up and left calmly but surprisingly quickly.

When we got to the cars, fifty yards down the hill at the road, we all asked, "What's wrong? What's the problem?"

The ranger who had been sitting back at the car said, "While you were sitting up there singing, we saw these green lights floating down the hillside toward the graveyard. They floated down to where you guys were sitting and standing, and they mingled in among you like they were part of the party. They weren't flashlights or anything; maybe a dozen of them were milling around you."

We were kind of skeptical, but the deadpan looks on these guy's faces convinced us. We drove back toward Philmont and talked about it."There were two levels of light," they explained, "some about as high as your chest, and some up around your heads."

That was when we began to realize it. Miners would have two kinds of lights: lanterns held at chest height and carbide lamps on their hard hats. Those of us actually in the graveyard never saw them, only the guys at the cars down the hill, but we knew that it must have been the miners coming home from the mine to sing and have a drink with the living, just as they had done three-quarters of a century before.

17   Senath Light

In the Bootheel of Missouri, at the small town of Senath, there is a ghost light. We got some directions on how to get there: you turn off the pavement at a certain point, drive a certain distance down a gravel road, cross a couple of bridges, then you're out in a soybean field and you come to a corner where there's an old, gnarled tree with a lot of character.

We knew the tree the minute we saw it in the dusk-light; it was a tree you might see in a horror film. You take another left, go down to another bridge, and park on the bridge. The hollow sounds echoing up from the old wooden bridge made the place pretty scary just to begin with. Real or imagined, the creaks and groans of the wooden bridge heightened our awareness as we waited for the light.

Then we saw the lights far ahead of us. There are all the usual explanations: swamp gas, lights at some distant airport, but these lights didn't look anything like that. They drifted slowly toward us, fairly high up, yellow-white in color, moving about above the road and the fields. Five of us sat and watched them come closer and closer. Then the bridge noises and the slow approach of the lights combined to give us all the excitement we had been looking for that night.

We left.

In reverse.

Quickly.

18   Ghost Light in Red

On the outskirts of Jonesboro, Arkansas, there is a mysterious grave haunted by a ghostly light of a very rare nature and color. College boys at A.S.U. [Arkansas State University] often take their dates to "park" beside the cemetery, where they can scare their dates with the obviously true story that explains the ghostly light.

The area is lonely and secluded, and many old stones and monuments rise high into the night among dark, twisted trees and sinister shrubbery. The ghostly light is easy to spot: unique in all the ghostlore, this light is red! You see, it's the grave of a prostitute buried almost a century ago.

The white monument is an obelisk, standing tall in the midst of other smaller stones that are more modern. The brazen hussy won't be still even in death, because if you park just in the right place, near a moss-covered monument carved from marble in the shape of a tree-trunk felled by the Grim Reaper, you can catch a glimpse of a pale red light, glowing from the orb at the top of the obelisk.

[The teller adds: and you must be careful to keep your date's attention on the graveyard, because if she looks directly opposite the graveyard on the other side of the road, she will notice the tall radio transmitter tower with the huge red light on it. The ghostly light is a romantic hoax.]

19 Ball Lightning

You know, I've never told anyone this until tonight, because I never heard of ball lightning before. I live right by the Illinois [River in northwest Arkansas], and my bedroom window looks out on the river. One night in the summer, when I was real young [about 1953], I was looking out the window and I saw a ball of white light come down out of the sky, fast, but not very fast, and it came down like this [she described a concave arc] over the water.

It flew right down the middle of the water, following the river, about three feet above the water, right down the middle of the river. It was about two feet in diameter, and it was white. I thought it was a ghost.

20 Ball of Fire

One night Grandma and Grandpa had gotten in the buggy to go somewhere, and as they drove along, there was a mild storm going on, but not real close. There was some rain falling, and when they got to the bridge that had to be crossed in order to get to town, a ball of fire came rolling down the river toward them.

They were scared bad. They had never seen a fireball, but Grandpa told me what it looked like: it was big, it was yellow and orange, and it rolled like a bowling ball down the river toward them. They turned around and went back to the house, they were so scared.

The next morning when they went to make the crossing again, the bridge had washed out.

21   The Lights in the Nursing Home

We were talking about strange lights: I saw some unusual ones when I worked at the nursing home here in town. At [this] nursing home, there are three small lights at night before someone dies. Small, little, round lights, a group of three. I had never really thought very much about the story. Apparently it goes all the way back to [the previous owners of the home]. This went on then, and when [the current owners] took it over, they didn't like rumors about their nursing home, and they told all the employees that rumors and gossip like that would not be tolerated and anyone caught spreading rumors or gossip like that would be fired.

Once or twice I had caught a glimpse of something out of the corner of my eye, but not anything I could pin down. Usually someone else would see it, too. It could be anywhere in the nursing home. It could be down the hall [from a patient who later died], in the room, or even over the bed. And usually after the lights had been seen, within the next twenty-four hours, someone would pass away. And the deaths always seemed to come in groups of three. Usually the lights were in close contact to the person who would die. A lot of times they would just be seen down the hall, but several times they were in the room or actually over the bed when they were seen.

22   Ball of Fire II

At Nacogdoches [Texas] out by the Old North Church graveyard, the local people have seen a ball of fire run along above the ground near the graves shortly after a new burial. The ball of fire always runs along barbed-wire fences or hog-wire fences, never along the road itself. They say it's the spirits of the newly dead, complaining about their lot.

23   The Texarkana Light

During the War Between the States, a Confederate soldier came home looking for his family. He had deserted having heard that his home had been raided. He went upstairs in the dark and discovered his family all murdered by jayhawkers. He found them when he lit a candle and raised it high to look around. He killed himself with his saber.

There is a ghostly light in the window still.

A casual acquaintance took me and a friend out on the dark road to see this light. We parked at the modern home of the land owner, within fifty feet of the empty old house, and as the driver went up, politely, to tell the occupants that we had come to see the ghost light, I looked over at the dark, empty dwelling from the past. There it was: a ghostly fluorescence in an upstairs window! It rose into view, then lowered back out of sight, almost like a candle raised as a signal to someone outside. I had never seen anything like it before.

It didn't look like a candle—but then, what else was it?

24   The Big Thicket Light

The Texans call the area "The Big Thicket." Between the Trinity River and the Neches River, around the town of Saratoga in Jefferson County, near the Old Bragg Road, the Texans see "The Big Thicket Light."

As you can tell from its name, the area is dense with undergrowth and was an ideal hideout during the early period of Texas history, and during and after the Civil War. The only clearings through the Thicket are the roads, the railroad right-of-ways, and occasional clearings where hunters gather around pine knot fires to tell the ghostly tales of the region after a long day's hunt.

The story has it that a jayhawker [used here to mean "union sympathizer"] was killed in a burn-out at the town of Kaiser by Confederates seeking out "slackers" who were avoiding military service to the Confederacy. The man ran burning from the house and ran into the Thicket, setting some of the underbrush on fire. His ghost still walks the Thicket as a small ball of flame.

When the Santa Fe Railroad came through, the ghost light often followed the tracks. When the tracks were pulled up in 1934, the light followed the empty railbed. After the road through the area was paved in 1952, the light was seen more often as more passers-by looked into the Thicket on dark nights and watched the ghostly light moving slowly in the undergrowth.

25 The Miami Spooklight

On a dark, foggy night one autumn just outside of Miami [Oklahoma], a woman sent her daughter out to look for the cows and drive them back to the lot. This was at the turn of the century, so the daughter took a lighted lantern with her to cut the fog. The girl never came back. The mother became frightened and began to search for the girl about midnight. She also carried a lantern.

She searched all night and never found the daughter, but the cattle were scattered across the rolling hills. The mother continued to search, night after night, insane with grief. When she died of remorse, her spirit continued to walk on foggy nights in the fall. She can still be seen, or her lantern can, on cold, foggy nights. I have seen the light; it's yellow like a lantern, and it swings just a little bit as if the ghost were carrying it while walking.

26 Spooklight at Hornet

In 1886, settlers about eleven miles southwest of Joplin, Missouri, began to see a ghostly light. It was blamed on the ghost of a Quapaw Indian (the Quapaw Agency was at Seneca a few miles away) looking for his lost lover, who had committed suicide rather than give in to her father's wish that she marry a man of his choosing instead of the young Quapaw. The light scared some settlers so badly they abandoned their farms and moved away. Today, the light is called the Hornet Spook Light for the settlement a few miles away.

27 Hornet Burial Ground

I used to know an old Cherokee man who ran a liquor store just outside of Seneca [Missouri], south of Joplin, about where [U. S. Highways] 71 and 66 cross. This Indian man told me that when the road was cut through the area, they disturbed an Indian burial ground near Hornet. Those [spook] lights you see started being seen about the time the graves were disturbed.

The lights are the spirits of those disturbed burials, wandering in search of their scattered parts.

28 The Split Hornet Light

Years ago, when I was quite young, I had just gotten out on my own, and was working at a job in Joplin [Missouri]. A young man that I had been seeing came to me one evening and said, "You've got to come see this."

He said he wanted me to see the spooklight south of Joplin. I assumed that it must be...an excuse, you know. We were sitting parked at the side of the road with the lights off, and as we were talking and cuddling, a very bright, white light came up behind the car. It was beautiful! It was glowing white with blue fringes. It came directly toward the trunk, and when it got to the car it split in two and slowly passed by us on either side of the car, up about as high as the windows. It made no sound at all!

When it reached the hood, it rejoined and went on down the road.

29 The Still Hornet Light

When I was in high school, a whole bunch of my buddies and I decided one night, girls and guys, to go up to Hornet [Missouri] to see the spooklight. One of us knew the way from up in our corner of Oklahoma, closest to Missouri, and they wanted all of us to go up and look, and check on it.

We saw the spooklight do something it hardly ever does, just sit absolutely still. It was yellow, shaded toward orange.

It was about the size of a basketball and it was sitting in an open field about three feet off the ground.

Very quietly, from about two hundred feet out, we encircled the light, all the way around it. Some fools will tell you that what causes the spooklight is headlights from the Will Rogers Turnpike (in Oklahoma), but when I was in high school, the Turnpike hadn't been built yet. And the light is seen in the hollows between the hills; there's not any way that the intelligence this light displays in its movement could be headlights.

Very quietly, speaking to each other, we all took one step forward, then another, then another. The light was just hanging there, three feet off the ground. We all took one more step and when we got about fifty feet from it, it winked out.

The light immediately appeared a hundred yards away, off to one side, just hanging in mid-air. At that point, a lot of us had reached our tolerance and we left.

30 Ghost Light Along the Chisos

Along the Rio Bravo del Norte, which we call the Rio Grande, near the Big Bend in the river, there is a ghostlight that moves among the Chisos Mountains. The Mexicans call it *la luz espantosa.*

If a cowboy is lost in the twisting, turning valleys and watersheds of the Chisos Mountains and singing to himself as he searches for the way back to camp, he may hear the echo of his song go on longer than the verse he was singing. The ghostly singing will echo off the cliffs and around the chasms.

Then he will see a ghost light moving along at the level of a rider on horseback, as if the rider were carrying a lantern. He may imagine he hears a woman singing, but then a lonely cowboy often imagines that, even when a coyote howls. He follows her, whatever she may be, with her light.

Some cowboys say the light will lead the cowpoke to safety. Others say it will lead him off a cliff in the blackness of night. Even if the cowboy dies, he dies happy and hopeful, better than dying in the desert sun the next day. But I like to think the ghost light leads the cowboy out safely.

Singing as it goes.

31   *Bayou Bourleau*

At the Bayou Bourleau, just beside the plantation house Pointe Chrétienne, there is the ghost of a girl who was killed on the bridge over the bayou. She appears in a white shroud. Sometimes she is called a *feu follé,* because she glows like fire.

She stands still on the bridge as you approach her and you can get very close to her, but if you try to touch her, she will disappear.

32   *The Marfa Lights*

Marfa, Texas, was established in 1881 as a water stop on the old Texas and New Orleans Railroad. In 1883, someone driving cattle between Alpine and Marfa saw the most famous ghost light of them all. For over a century, the Marfa lights have been seen moving slowly along the ground.

One story says that back in the 1850s, West Texas was just beginning to be settled and people were very scattered. One winter, a bad blizzard blew in and a rancher who had not been prepared, went out to get firewood. His family became worried when he did not return, and they went out with lanterns to search for him. None of them ever returned to the house, and the Marfa lights are the family out looking for the rancher.

33   *Lights at Silverton*

I have seen the phenomenon of lights in the old graveyard at Silverton, Colorado. It's an ancient cemetery [the teller later explained that he meant "very old" by that] from the heyday of mining in Silverton. The mines were abandoned long ago, but the cemetery remains.

I was standing up on a kind of a nob of a hill above the cemetery, and I saw between twenty and seventy softball-sized lights. They're white and they rise from just above the grave and they rise up to about fifteen or twenty feet in the air, and then they go back down, and then they rise again.

How many there were fluctuated, and how fast they were moving fluctuated, too.

34 *Ball of Fire III*

At Lucero, they say a woman was killed by dogs. The dogs were demons working for the Devil, and they got hungry, so they killed her. Her spirit is still there, and she is angry. She comes up from Hell and rolls around as a ball of flame. She only comes out when the moon is full. They only come out then, you know.

35 *Ball of Fire IV*

At this old house that was abandoned, some people were going by in a wagon and they saw light in the house. They went to look, but nobody was in there. Then a big ball of fire, a *brasero,* came out of the chimney and rolled at them. They really ran. And as they left, they saw sparks coming out of the chimney.

Ghosts of the Roadways

36 Raw Head and Bloody Bones

Deep in the wooded hills and hollows of the Ozark Mountains of Missouri there lived an old conjuring woman who knew all the herbs and roots and cures and magical spells. Everybody in the hollow came to her for remedies, but she only had one friend: a lean, mean wild razorback hog. The old boar came by her house and ate her kitchen garbage; he ate so many of her leftover roots and discarded magical potions that he got to where he could walk and talk like a man.

The old woman and the old boar got along fine for many years, but one year in October, at hog-slaughtering time, a lazy hillbilly who didn't have any hogs rounded up his neighbors'. He must have rounded up the conjuring woman's pet, too, and taken him to the Hog-Scald Hollow where all the neighbors had gathered to shoot the hogs, cut their throats to bleed them out, and hang them up for gutting. After gutting a carcass, they would scald it with boiling water and scrape the hair off. After the meat was ready for the smokehouse, nothing was left but the bloody bones in a pile at the bluff wall. Even the hogs' heads were skinned and taken back to the house to boil and make souse.

When all the meat to be smoked was loaded into burlap bags, and loaded into the wagon, and the heads laid alongside, and the sun was going down, everyone would leave the hollow. The last one to leave was the lazy thief, looking about for one last morsel to scavenge. As he rode off in his wagon, the skinned head of the old conjuring woman's pet bounced out into the dirt road.

The skinned head spoke: "Bloody bones, get up and dance!"

Back at Hog-Scald Hollow, the bloody bones of the conjuring woman's hog got up and danced around. The bones got back together and ran down the road and collected up the head. The ghastly creature followed the wagon to the lazy thief's house.

Raw Head and Bloody Bones went to all the critters in the deep woods and borrowed things to wear. He borrowed the panther's fangs; he borrowed the bear's claws; he borrowed the raccoon's tail.

At the cabin, the old man and the old woman were in bed asleep. Suddenly there was a noise like something falling into the fireplace. The fire flared up and the old man awoke.

The old man got up to see what was the matter. He looked and looked but couldn't find anything amiss. Then he looked up the chimney.

"Land o' Goshen," said the old man, "what have you got those big old eyes for?"

"To see your grave..." said the deep hollow voice up the chimney. The old man ran and hid under the bed. After a few minutes he got curious and came back and looked up the chimney again.

"Land o' Goshen," he said, "what have you got those great big claws for?"

"To dig your grave..." said the deep, dark voice. The old man ran and hid under the bed again. After a few minutes he got curiouser and curiouser. He came out and went back to the chimney.

"Land o' Goshen," he said, "what have you got that big bushy tail for?"

"TO SWEEP YOUR GRAVE..." said the rumbling rolling voice. The old man ran and hid under the washtub. After a long time he got so curious he couldn't stand it any more. He came back out and looked up the chimney one last time at the raw head and the bloody bones.

"Land o' Goshen," he said, "what have you got those long sharp teeth for?"

"TO EAT YOU UP!" said the Raw Head and Bloody Bones, and it came down the chimney and carried off the lazy hillbilly and stole his horse, too.

They never saw the old man again, but they saw Raw Head and Bloody Bones wearing the old man's shirt and overalls riding on the stolen horse. It carried its old raw head in its hand, up high against the full moon. Old Raw Head and Bloody Bones!

37   *The Guard at San Marcos Bridge*

The bridge over the San Marcos River on old U.S. Highway 80 is guarded by a ghost. He wears high boots and grey pants held up by suspenders, an underwear shirt, and a Confederate cap. He stands at the parade-rest guard stance so many Confederates used, leaning on his rifle, guarding the bridge.

Local legend says that brothers who volunteered for the South during the War Between the States swore to return home, dead or alive. The one who came home alive is buried and gone. The one who died in battle is still on duty, one-and-one-quarter centuries later.

38   *White Wolf*

Between the Clear Fork and the Double Mountain Fork of the Brazos River, U.S. 180 follows one branch of the Old Southern Trail to California. Fort Phantom Hill was built to guard that trail across the empty grasslands and low mesas of Central Texas. Hundreds of wagons passed Westward along the trails, and many wagons and inhabitants vanished, the prey of marauders, wild animals, or disease and starvation. Thousands of unmarked graves must lie along those trails. And one that is marked by legend.

Among the many wagon trains that passed, one wagon slowed and stopped to wait for death. A young boy was ill with a high fever, and the family camped to spend the boy's last days. One night, the boy asked to sleep outside on the ground instead of in the wagon. His fever was so high and he was so hot, the mother finally consented.

Sometime after midnight, the boy awoke, feverish, and looked toward the dark mesa that overhung the camp. High, high up on the mesa's rim sat a ghostly white form with red, red eyes. A long, low howl echoed down the stone incline. The boy fell asleep.

The moon set and the night grew deeply dark. Only the pale light of the stars lit the camp when the boy awoke again. Across the dead campfire sat a great white shape with red, red eyes. At first the boy was afraid, but the figure never moved and gradually the youth decided it was just some laundry laid out on the water barrel. He fell asleep again.

One last time, some before dawn, the boy awoke.

The thing sat beside the boy's bedroll, looking down at him with red, red eyes.

"It's just a dog," thought the boy with a smile, "a big, white dog."

The great creature lowered its muzzle to the boy's face and gently licked his fevered brow. The boy laughed and closed his eyes for the last time. A long, low growl began outside the wagon and rose to an unearthly howl that climbed the mesa walls and rang out over the prairie.

The father leapt up and grabbed his rifle, but by the time he was down from the wagon, the camp was empty and the boy was dead. They buried him after dawn under the prairie mound beside the camp.

As the wagon rolled away, a huge white wolf watched it go—a wolf with red, red eyes.

Through the years the grave was seen by many passing travellers; one wagon even stopped and saw small white bones sticking out of the sand. When the men went over to investigate, an enormous albino wolf leapt over the prairie mound and sent them scattering with a snarl.

The legend grew. Some settlers said the wolf guarded the grave. Others said it was the wolf that killed the boy. But finally, the legend came to say that the ghost of the boy was the wolf himself. The white wolf.

With the red, red eyes.

39 *The Ghostly Battle*

Most folks don't know it, but during the War Between the States, volunteers from California went East and fought, some for the Confederacy, some for the Union. A lot of volunteers went from Northern California. After the war, many of the dead were transported back and buried here. On the winding road between Redman and Elkhorn, there is a little cemetery in the valley where the war is still fought, day and night, by the ghosts of those brave volunteers.

High up in the mountains, the graveyard holds both Confederate and Union dead. A precarious, crooked road works its way down off one mountain, through the valley, past the graveyard, and up the other valley wall. From the overlook on the road, high above the grass-covered graves, many drivers swear to have seen a battle going on in the valley below.

I was just a young man, twenty-five or thirty years old, just out of the armed services and I had a truck-driving job delivering machine parts between Redman and Elkhorn and other places. One day I came up the side of the mountain with the loaded truck laboring, and as I came around the horseshoe bend at the overlook, I chanced to look down at the graveyard far below me. I had heard the legend that if you saw the battle in progress, you wouldn't live to climb the other side of the valley; you'd be killed on the twisting road going down. I didn't believe that part of the legend. But even though I'd heard about the battle all my life, I wasn't prepared for how real it all looked.

Because, there was the battle, going on—and these didn't look like ghosts, these looked like flesh-and-blood men, easily a hundred soldiers, fighting on one side or the other. I could see the puffs of smoke coming out of their rifle-barrels; I could see the sunlight glinting off their guns, their uniform buttons; I could see them, but I couldn't hear a thing. It was completely silent.

But a fierce battle was taking place between men in blue uniforms and men in grey. I pulled over to the side of the road at the overlook, stopped the truck, and sat there and shook for several minutes, not daring to look again. And then I reminded myself of the rest of the legend, that "you wouldn't make it to the other side," and that I was now probably going to be killed if I didn't go back the way I'd come, and back around another way.

After a long wait, I started the truck and pulled out down the hill toward the valley, against the warning in the legend, driving at five miles an hour, around the sweeping curve to the other side of the valley. As I got even with the graveyard, I dared to look.

At that moment the sun was setting. There were no ghosts in the graveyard, just old, weather-worn stones. I drove to the next town, parked the truck, and I never drove that road again.

40 *The Head on the High Road*

There was a young Spanish *caballero* in the regiment at Santa Fe who was proud but lonely. All the other *caballeros* had ladies, but not he. It was the custom to hold a dance on the last night of each month for all the regiment, and for each dance, one of the *caballeros* would be the host and his lady the hostess. It was the lonely *caballero's* turn to host the dance for October. He had no one to serve as his hostess, and the dance was only weeks away.

He had noticed a lovely young *señorita* who ate every day at Sena Plaza; she was the daughter of one of the Sena family. She ate alone at a table every day, and she was beautiful. He dressed in his best uniform to meet her one day. She had a cup of coffee, and it was half-empty. He came to her table and asked if he might serve her more coffee; in this way he hoped to gain permission to join her. She agreed. He poured her cup full and joined her. She smiled but did not speak throughout the meal. When she had finished, he pulled out her chair for her, and she left without a farewell. Every day for a week he offered to pour her coffee, each day she left without a word.

On Sunday, after Mass, he approached her family to ask if he could escort her to the regimental dance. They ignored him and rode away in their carriage. At lunch the next day, he returned, offered to pour her coffee, she agreed, and as he seated himself, he saw her handkerchief laid on the table. He decided to take it so she would think she had lost it and returning it, he could gain her favor. He took her handkerchief when she wasn't looking, and she departed without it. He went to her house that night, but the servant who answered the door refused to admit him.

He joined her the next day and tried to bring up the "missing" handkerchief. She said she was not missing anything, and after that she said nothing else. Another week went by without any success. Every attempt failed. At last, he resorted to the last remedy. While he was drinking in the cantina, a friend advised him to go to the two *brujas* who lived in the Oldest House. He gathered all his money and polished his boots and went to see the witches.

Up the narrow, dark street was an adobe house with a low, crooked door. He knocked, and finally an old woman answered, an old woman with white porcelain skin, fragile, and very old.

"What do you want that you cannot leave us in peace?" she demanded.

He explained that he needed to see the witches and why.

"We have been called many things," said the old woman, "*viejas* [old], *feas* [ugly], but never *brujas!* How dare you call us witches?"

He told them he was in desperate need, and the woman admitted him in an apparent change of heart. Behind the door, as she closed it, he saw another old woman cooking at a great *calderón* [cooking pot] over a smokeless fire. Behind her was a wooden case filed with different vials and bottles. He explained his problem again, and called her *bruja*, again.

"Don't call me *bruja*," she said. "If you have to call me anything, call me *abuelita* [little grandmother]. Love brings nothing but trouble. But for all those coins, I will give you this." She walked to the case and picked out a tall, thin purple vial, and she blew the dust off of it and cackled.

"You can take this vial and give me all your coins, or you can leave with your wealth and leave this vial here. Either way, I promise you, you will still have a problem. There are no guarantees in life."

The soldier took the vial and gave her the coins. He left at once. The next afternoon he met the *señorita* at Sena Plaza and when he poured her coffee, he held the vial beneath her handkerchief and poured its contents into the cup as he flaunted the kerchief to her. She drank the coffee and snatched the *pañuelo* from him; she stood up and left with a look of contempt that told him she never wanted to see him again. The contents of the vial seemed not to have worked.

It was All Saints Eve, and the *caballero* was humiliated to have no hostess for the dance. He marched back to the house of the Sena family and forced his way past the servant to see if the potion had worked. The *señorita* slammed the door in his face. Her feelings for him were unchanged, but more intense. He marched back to the Oldest House and pounded on the door.

He had been drunk the night before, bragging to his friends in the cantina; now he had nothing. He wanted revenge. His sword rattled in its scabbard as he knocked. It reminded him that he should defend his honor with his sword. The old woman opened the door and looked at him with such a glare. He drew his sword and demanded his money back.

"Give me back the vial and I will give you back your coins."

He pulled the vial from his waistcoat pocket and presented it to her.

"This is empty. Give me what was in it and I'll give you the coins."

The *caballero* screamed that the witches were powerless.

"I never claimed to be a witch," said the old woman. "You called me a witch. I told you there are no guarantees in life!"

The *caballero* held his sword to the old woman's throat and demanded his coins. Out of nowhere a long knife flew through the air. Did the other woman throw it? Or was it witchcraft?

The knife took off the *caballero*'s head. The head fell to the street, and rolled slowly down the sloping street, down toward the plaza, making a ghastly thumping noise as it rolled. Its eyes were open and its mouth was ready to scream.

And now today in Santa Fe, on Hallowe'en Night, if you stand by the Oldest House, you can hear the head rolling down to the plaza.

41 *The Headless Caballero*

Around the herb shop of Delfinio Luján, on Galisteo Street, they tell the tale of the headless *caballero* of Alto Street. He lost his head to two witches when they sold him a love potion that didn't work. Now he rides his fine horse up and down Alto Street, along the river, looking for his head.

He brandishes his sword at you if he sees you, and acts as if he'll cut off your head, too, for spite, for staring at him.

He never has found his head.

42 La Malogra

Then there's *la Malogra [la Malhora,* or *mala hora,* the bad hour]. You see her when you are walking at a crossroads and someone is going to die. She foretells death. She takes on human form and sometimes to see her drives you insane. Sometimes she wears a sheepskin, like the *borregueros* wear. She is like *la LLorona.* She is a bad thing.

43 Ghost Girl of the Mimbres

The old-timers say there's a lonely gal who rides the Mimbres and lures cowboys astray. They say she was a pretty lady in life, but one who lived so far out that she seldom saw anyone but her brothers and the ranch hands. And that, as the old-timers say, would be like kissing your sister.

One day she caught a glimpse of a handsome rider, and she followed him, hoping to find out whereabouts he lived. He took a sharp turn in the deep canyons, and she lost him, and she lost her way. The ranch hands found her months later, dead beneath a mesquite tree.

When the cowpokes see a well-dressed lady on the Mimbres now, a pretty Anglo lady in turn-of-the-century duds, they know not to follow her. She'll lead you into the twisting canyons and you'll never come out. Unless you come out riding with her, forever, on the Mimbres.

44 La LLorona

People of Santa Fe have always celebrated the end of *Zozobra* [Old Man Gloom] with a fiesta where we burn him [in effigy], but now the people of Santa Fe are interested in a true tale or belief of the people. She is *la LLorona* [The Weeping Woman].

Once this woman was a widow, and she had two children. She fell in love with a rich nobleman, but he wasn't interested in her because he didn't want to have to raise her two children by her first man. So she took the children to the *acequia* [irrigation ditch] and drowned them, and let their bodies float downstream. When she told the nobleman that she was free of the children, he was horrified. Now he really didn't want anything to do with her.

She went back to the *acequia,* looking for her children. They were gone. This was a long time ago. Now she continues to wander the valleys and weep and wail over the loss of her children. She warns drunkards to mend their ways and tells people to go back to church if they've quit going for some reason.

She's like the bogeyman, and she's the conscience of those who don't have a conscience anymore. She is *la LLorona.*

45 *La LLorona II*

That's *la LLorona,* you know [the teller gestures at a painting in the Museum of Fine Arts]. She comes at night to the people who are out too late or who are doing bad things and makes them stop. She wears this *rebozo* [shawl], and when she has warned you to stop what you're doing wrong, if you don't listen to her, she takes off her *rebozo* and she is a skull. Sometimes someone will shoot at her and try to kill her, but she turns into a snake to get away in the grass. You can't kill her anyway, because she's already dead. She murdered her own children, and now you see her by waterways because she drowned them. The *abuelos* and *abuelas* [grandfathers and grandmothers] use her to scare the little children and make them obey, but grown men see her, too. I've never seen her, but I know people who have. That's what people say. But it all sounds like *pozole* [hominy stew] to me.

46 *Hitchhiker at Tierra Amarilla*

There is a ghostly hitchhiker on the road up near Tierra Amarilla. An anglo boy who drank too much and drove too fast got drunk one night at a party. He tried to drive home and crashed his truck into the solid granite wall where the road had been dynamited through the mountain. His father had a grotto built into the granite, with a scene of the Holy Family in small statues, there at the spot where the wreck took place. Every year on the anniversary of the boy's death, the father goes there and lights vigil candles.

When I was a little girl, young women who might be driving alone, to a dance or something, on the anniversary of the boy's death, might drive by the grotto late at night. They would see the ghostly image of the boy, standing out on the road, trying to flag them down.

Everyone always said that if the girls had been drinking or doing things they should not have been doing, the sight of the ghost would make them slam on their brakes [to keep from hitting him] and they would crash into the granite wall right where he had been killed years before.

That kept a lot of the young girls from going out at night.

47 *Booger Dog*

There is a ghost dog that walks by night in the old section of Waco [Texas]. He is bigger than a dog, almost as big as a mule, and black as the night that he comes out in. Some folks see the ghost dog when they've been haughty to their elders or when they've been lying or cheating, but some folks see him just because they're out alone on a dark night.

He'll jump out and scare a lone walker and send him scurrying. He'll step out of the woods in front of a mule or wagon-team and they'll stop dead in their tracks. He's even been known to jump on the hood of a car, and the weight puts the frame down on the tires and ruins them.

Folks that know better get home before two [a.m.] if they know what's good for them. But if you can cross the Brazos [River] when you see him, you'll be safe: ghosts can't cross running water.

48   The Headless Outlaw

Two Texas Rangers, W. A. A. "Bigfoot" Wallace and Creed Taylor, used to tell the tale of the headless rider, now known across Texas from San Antonio to Waco. Wallace had come to Texas in 1836, and became a Ranger after his brother was killed at the Goliad Massacre and the new State of Texas needed to track down outlaws with a newly created law enforcement agency.

One of the outlaws in those early days had a price on his head. The reward was for bringing in the outlaw, dead or alive, for identification. One Ranger caught up to this outlaw, killed him in a fair gunfight, and cut off the head to transport back for the reward, because he was too lazy to take the whole corpse. This practice was frowned on by the Rangers and especially by the ghost of the outlaw.

Sometimes the headless outlaw is seen riding the trails between the Brazos and the Trinity [Rivers], searching for his head. Sometimes the headless outlaw is seen riding with his severed head, which he has dug up from its ignominious grave, tied to the saddle horn, and the eyes of the head glow with the fires of Hell, where the soul has presumably spent some time in the Devil's calaboose.

Sometimes, when the headless rider is seen, cattlemen are heard to remark, "Why doesn't he go on back down to Hell? It's cooler there than it is here in Texas."

49   Ghostly Express

At Hanover, in northern Kansas, was the old Hollenberg stop on the Pony Express trail to Sacramento. The Pony Express only ran for eighteen months, but in that time many riders died or disappeared. They say you can still hear the faint sound of hooves, like distant thunder, and the warning cry of "Hello-o-o-o" that meant a rider was coming in and the station master should have a fresh horse ready. Some of them [the riders] are still riding, refusing to believe that they were cut down by a bullet or an arrow over a hundred years ago.

50 *The Lady of White Rock Lake*

There's the story of a young girl who appears regularly at White Rock Lake in Dallas. She is wet and alone and is given a ride by an unsuspecting motorist. She is taken to an apartment, at her request, and says good night; then she disappears, either while still seated in the car or just after stepping out. A wet spot on the upholstery proves that she was not a hallucination.

The motorist asks around among the apartment residents, and they do not know anything about her. Sometimes—for this has happened very often, we are told—the girl tells a tale of terror about having been left at the lake by a boy who tried to drown her.

(It may be that the girl, who is often described as wearing a white dress, died so long ago that no one at the apartment building lived there when she did, or that the apartment building is built on the site of her former home and she disappears when she, as a ghost, recognizes that her home is no longer there.)

Haunted Houses

51a *The Ghost Smokes A Pipe*

Have you heard the story about the ghost who smokes a pipe?
In a big, old brick house down by the San Antonio River, there
lived a young Army Air Corps pilot named Sidney Brooks. He
was learning to be a pilot before World War I. He died in a
crash. Brooks Air Force Base is named after him.

Some people say the young pilot used to smoke a pipe.

Every family to live in the house since 1917 has sometimes... when the person is sure he or she is alone...smelled
the smoke from a pipe. Even when no one who smokes a pipe
lives in the house...they smell that sweet pipe smoke.

Sometimes, on Halloween, small pieces of furniture seem
to move on their own. Sometimes people who live there think
they see someone out of the corner of their eye...someone
dressed in old-fashioned clothes. Perhaps a young man with
a moustache.

Maybe it's the young pilot.

The one who smokes a pipe.

51b *Ghost Who Smoke Pipe*

(The story "The Ghost Smokes A Pipe" was told in San Antonio by
   deaf clients of the Southwest Center for the Hearing Impaired.
   One way it might be told from one hearing-impaired person to

another is by following this written American Sign Language version.)

Up-until-now you hear finish story name Ghost Who Smoke Pipe?

Long ago [use two hands and make the sign slowly] young man airplane pilot live house [point with index finger as if to indicate where] near San Antonio River.

Man name (fingerspell) S-i-d-n-e-y B-r-o-o-k-s [repeat SB to designate his name in the rest of the story.]

Before World War One start SB learn fly airplane [gaze upwards as if you see the plane overhead]. Later (long time) SB fly-plane crash SB die. B-r-o-o-k-s (fingerspell) Air Force Base here [point to indicate here] San Antonio.

Name why? Young man name S-i-d-n-e-y- B-r-o-o-k-s.

Up until SB die he [point as if he were present] smoke pipe [classifier]. SB die finish. Now (present time) family live there [point as you did before to where the house might stand] same house SB live before die.

Sometime family live there [indicate] and no person smoke and sometime person alone [indicate] sometime pipe smoke [slow the signs down and look around as if you smell something] smell.

[Sign very close to your body and dart your eyes about as if you were now frightened by the story you are telling.] Sometime Hallowe'en night chair move itself table move itself. Sometime people live house [indicate] think see person [dart your eyes to the right and back, as if you thought you saw someone] person clothes past [sign past with both hands to indicate long ago].

Maybe [pause] young man who live past [sign with two hands to indicate long ago] fly airplane who [slow gestures down] smoke pipe [let the sign for pipe seem to float in the air as if it were floating away].

52 *The Ghost Door*

My grandpa and grandma bought a house over in Newton County not too many years back. An old man had died in one of the bedrooms, and Grandpa left that room more or less empty, just for storage. It had a solid wooden door that wouldn't stay closed. He would shut the door every night, and the plunger would click, but about midnight the plunger would click again and the door would swing slowly open.

The hinges needed oiling, and the door would creak.

Some nights it scared Grandma and Grandpa pretty bad.

Grandpa decided to oil the hinges and put one of those screen-door latches with an eye-hook on the door. He put the eye-hook into the frame and shut the door. It clicked the same as always, and he latched the latch.

About midnight the plunger clicked and woke Grandpa up.

Then he heard the latch drop against the door, loose from its eyehook.

Then he heard the door creak open, the same as always.

He got up the next morning and unscrewed the latch and eye-hook and threw them away. He left the door standing ajar that night and every night after that, and they were never awakened again.

53 *The Ghost at Hughes*

At Hughes, Arkansas, two brothers, James and John, lived in a house that they had been told was haunted. The previous owner, an old man, claimed that his dead wife haunted the house. When he died, the house went up for sale. After the brothers bought the house, the ghost of the wife was seen for the first time by anyone other than the old man. She always wore a long, white gown; she had died young and was very pretty for a ghost.

One afternoon the brothers came home from working in the soybean fields, and they were walking toward the refrigerator for a soda. A friend of theirs who had come home with them looked down a hallway from the kitchen, and he saw a woman pass by, and he dropped his drink. It scared him, because he knew the house should have been empty, and he asked James and John who was home besides them. They said, "Nobody's here," but he swore up and down that he'd seen a woman in a long white gown. That old boy left for home shortly after that.

Jim and John both just laugh about this story, because even though the house is haunted, they've lived there long enough to know this haunt wasn't going to hurt them. They'd become comfortable with the idea of a ghost in their house. Several times the ghost had appeared; they had seen her, other guests at the place had seen her. But finally even the brothers were scared by the lady in the white gown.

One day their father had come home. He thought his wife was around the house, and doing some work upstairs. He could hear her footsteps upstairs, and he called up, "I'm just going to get a sandwich and go back to the fields." His wife didn't answer, but he heard her moving around upstairs. In a few minutes he called up, "I'm going back out, now, honey." He could hear her rocking chair upstairs rocking. Then his wife walked in the front door. She'd gone to town and come back.

They ran upstairs and opened the door to the sewing room. The rocking chair was still rocking, but it was empty. That scared their father, and after that, the whole family was not so comfortable as they'd been before to share their home with a lady in a long, white gown.

54 *The Baker's Ghost*

Many years ago, my great-grandmother Klussman had a most extraordinary experience. Her family lived in a two-story house whose foundations rested directly on the ground, without a cellar or any underground rooms beneath it. In the front hall stood a great curving stairway that led to the bedrooms upstairs. One evening as she was leaving the parlor, having bidden Great-great-grandfather good night, she approached the stairway to ascend.

She stopped at the foot of the steps and looked down, catching hold of the front of her floor-length dress to lift it so she could climb the stairs. When she looked up to begin her ascent, she saw at the head of the stairs a ghostly white figure on the second floor landing, looking down at her!

The figure was entirely white, unnaturally tall, and spectral. It seemed to stand with its arms hanging at its sides; then, it raised its right arm, bending it at the elbow, and seemed to gesture downward toward her, as if telling her to go away.

She dropped the gatherings of her dress and ran back into the parlor; she brought her father into the hall, but the figure was gone. Great-great-grandfather seemed concerned but not at all afraid. Great-grandmother thought that perhaps he had not believed her story.

For many nights she climbed the stairs without incident.

Suddenly one night, for no apparent reason she could see, the figure returned. As before, she had stopped at the foot of the stairs to lift her dress front, and as she looked up to begin the ascent, the figure reappeared. This time he was very distinctly visible.

It was a man, dressed in a white baker's costume. He was not incredibly tall: his height was augmented by a high, white baker's or chef's hat. His face was calm, not at all threatening. He again gestured, but this time she could see more clearly what he meant. Starting with his arms at his sides, he raised his right arm, bending it at the elbow, and with a downward sweep of his arm, he pointed his index finger toward the earth.

Down...he seemed to say. Down...or perhaps, below.

He continued to slowly gesture as the young girl studied him. She turned and called to her father, but when she looked back up the ghost was gone.

Great-great-grandfather believed what Great-grandmother had told him, and he summoned the parish priest. After some discussion, when the priest had determined that the family had only lived there a few decades, and that the house rested directly on the earth, he suggested that they open the area beneath the stairs.

With the gardener's help, the three men opened the wall below the steps and found an empty cobwebbed space with a dirt floor. Digging there they found, three feet down, a very old skeleton. In the dark earth they removed, there were tiny white flakes of rotten fine linen. Above the head, figuring horizontally, they found the rusted and crushed wire frame of a baker's hat.

The priest took the bones to the ossuary and blessed them. The wall was closed up and the baker's ghost was never seen again.

55 *The Haunted House at Howe*

I was preaching one Sunday at Howe, and after the evening service some of the elders of that congregation were waiting for me in the back of the church, shuffling their feet and talking amongst themselves.

When everyone else was gone home, one of them approached me and said, "Brother John, I have a favor to ask of you."

I listened intently as he explained.

"One of our congregation owns a house in Howe, and he wants to sell it, but he can't. No one will buy it because everyone says it's haunted. In the middle of the darkest nights, folks riding by say they see ghostly lights in the dormer windows. We were wondering if you would spend the night in that house tonight and quell these rumors for me."

Well, I agreed; I got my pipe and my copy of *Railway Through the Word,* from which I was preaching that week, and blew out the lanterns. We loaded into two automobiles and drove to the house, which sat in a grove of live oaks. The house was two-and-a-half stories, long empty, and some of the windows were out. The lights of the automobiles gave me a brief view of the house before we parked. We sat about discussing the matter for several minutes, and the deacons announced that they would "stay out here and keep watch."

I put some Prince Albert in my pipe and puffed it up enough to see by, took my book, and went inside. The owner had told me about the stairs, where the ladder to the loft was, and so on. Pretty soon I was in the upper floor, which was a child's bedroom.

It was empty but for an old bedframe and a rocker gathering dust. Four windows looked out of the hipped roof, one to each point of the compass. The panes were mostly out, and some ragged gauze curtains hung there and about, but the room was dark except for the glow of my pipe.

I sat in the rocker and began to read, with my pipe upside down to read by. I guess I fell asleep, because the next thing I knew, the pipe dropped out of my mouth and hit the book in my lap. I jumped up and brushed the ashes off the book to keep from starting a fire, but the pipe was long since cold and the ashes dead. Then I began to realize something else.

With the pipe out, it should be dark. Instead it was lighter than before I'd sat down. I put down the book and put the cold pipe in my pocket and looked around the room. It was filled with a faint, flickering blue-white light—not the yellow light of a candle or the pure white of an electric bulb—a blue-white light that came from nowhere and flickered on the walls.

First I looked out the north window. It was dark all the way to Sherman. Out the east window, there were only live oaks. Out the south window, there was light toward McKinney, but nothing like the ghostly light in the room. Then I looked out the west window.

There in the distance, over the horizon, invisible from the ground, the Katy [Missouri, Kansas and Texas Railroad or M.K.T.—"Katy" for short] was rolling south from Oklahoma City to Fort Worth, making a big sweeping turn north of Denton. The big battery-electric headlamp of the train, sweeping both sides of the tracks, was shining in the windows and lighting up just the top floor.

The former occupants must have known, but on the street below the owner and passersby thought the light came from the loft.

I gathered up the book and made my way down to the street. I kicked the fender to wake the menfolks in the automobile and said, "Let's go home, boys. It's a train."

The house was sold the next day.

56 *The Healing Lady of Los Luceros*

The Spanish soldiers who camped at Cabezón pressed northward for Taos in their search for the Cities of Gold. They did not stop at Española along the way. They were off the regular trail, and they came to a mysterious three-story adobe building. No one knew how old it was, or who had built it, or why. The kitchen took up one-half of the ground floor and was tiled with Mexican tile. Some said it was built by Mexican Indians trying to reach Chaco Canyon, seeking refuge from the Spanish conquest of Mexico; others said a group of Spanish foot soldiers who had separated from their cavalry to become mercenaries and collect slaves had built it. When the young soldiers traveling to Taos found it, the building was deserted.

It was at the place called Los Luceros, and they came upon the adobe structure after nightfall. The third floor glowed in the darkness with light from windows and balconies. When the boys pushed open the heavy door and went inside the first floor, there was food cooking on the stove, even though there was no wood burning in the stove. The food was hot. They ate in the dark, for they could not find any candles or lamps, and they did not build a fire, for there was no wood in the kitchen.

The *capitán* wanted to find out what was upstairs. He and the scout went upstairs while the others remained below, watching them. The bottom stair was a single piece of wood with box stairs going up, and the stairs turn partway up; the *capitán* and the scout went out of sight, and they stopped talking. They stopped calling out. The soldiers couldn't hear them anymore.

When the *capitán* and the scout didn't come down, they sent up the cook and his helper. The cook took two wooden spoons and a piece of string and made a cross, and held it to his forehead as he walked up the stairs. When they were up the stairs, the helper stopped talking, and the cook became afraid, but he didn't look back. He walked all the way around the second floor, calling down to the soldiers below, and then he came back down alone. When he removed the wooden cross, it had left a brand on his forehead, and he was blind.

The cook started to tell them that when he went upstairs he saw a large room, and all the walls were lit. Because the *capitán,* the scout, and now the cook's helper had all vanished, they decided to send up the youngest boy holding a large cross, and with him others of the youngest soldiers with crosses. And instead of walking, they would go on their knees and recite the "Hail, Mary" as they went. Four young boys were picked, and they took crosses, and they left their swords below and went up, very scared, without their boots, in stockings only. At the top of the stairs, they said the "Hail, Mary" of the Cesarean Order, holding their crosses up to their foreheads in front of their faces. One brash boy looked out from behind his cross: the cross flew to the wall and embedded there, and the boy disappeared from the earth. The other boys saw it from behind their crosses. They walked on their knees back down the stairs in fear.

They had to leave without their missing commander, and they went on to Taos. There, at Taos, there were wounded men, and sick people, and some of the soldiers were eventually wounded, too. It was decided that the sick and wounded of Taos would return with this contingent of soldiers to the Sisters of the Holy Faith at Santa Fe for treatment, and only the well and strong would remain at the outpost at Taos. A storm drove the group to seek shelter, and it happened that they were at Los Luceros when the storm struck. The building glowed its beckoning light again, and the ill and wounded with their canes and crutches went inside.

They had knocked, and rung the heavy Mexican bell that hung there, called, and no one answered, and they had gone in. Once again, hot food was waiting. They ate and rested and rewrapped bandages, and whatever they needed to do. The soldiers, who knew about the house, went out to find shelter for the horses from the storm. Only the sick remained inside, and when the horses were hobbled, they found the heavy door locked: they could not get back in.

Looking through the windows, the soldiers saw a woman all in white, with white hair and a necklace of red roses, floating down the stairwell, glowing with light. She lifted each ill person and carried him effortlessly upstairs where they were out of sight. At morning, the door opened by itself, and the soldiers went in. The stove was cold, the kitchen dirty; in the other room, there was the travois and bandages and their baggage, but the people were gone.

On the second floor, all the canes and crutches had flown to the walls and embedded there, and they could not be removed. They heard a rattling on the third floor, above the *vigas* and *latias,* but there was no stairwell. Perhaps it was only birds, nesting from the storm the night before.

A week later, many leagues away, a pack train came upon a great group of people, whole and healthy but wandering and suffering from amnesia. They were led to Taos, where they were recognized, fed, cared for, and gradually came back to their memories. But they could not explain their incredible healing or their mysterious transport to far away.

Later, the territory became more settled and populated, and a chapel was built at Los Luceros, and eventually a coach house. Those who were afflicted would go to service in the chapel, go to the great kitchen and prepare a feast, and then take candles and go upstairs. They would sing hymns and pray and admire the canes and crutches in the walls, and they could hear rustling on the inaccessible floor above.

Then, in this century, one owner cut an opening and put stairs up to the third floor. There the owners found huge wooden trunks of woman's clothing—dresses, rebozos, all of it white—the garments of the glowing Lady of Los Luceros, who healed the sick.

57 Winchester Mansion

Fisher Winchester, the "Rifle King," had a son named William; he married a fine lady named Sarah, and they planned to have a long life together. He died not too long afterwards, and their only child died at birth. Sarah Winchester believed that their deaths were the curse on her for marrying into the family that had made its fortune manufacturing the rifle that had killed so many thousands of people in the West.

Sarah became afraid that the ghosts of all the dead people killed by Winchesters were coming to haunt her at her home, having been somehow denied their mansions in Heaven. And all these ghosts would move in when her mansion was finished. It was as if she were to "go to prepare a place" for them here on Earth, like Jesus said he had to "go to prepare a place" for his disciples in Heaven.

She found an uncompleted mansion in San José, California, and spent the rest of her life "completing" it so the ghosts could move in. The mansion had a hundred and sixty rooms, and she had carpenters constantly building blind stairways and whole rooms sealed off with furniture in them. Fireplaces were constructed without chimneys and windows were put in that opened onto blank walls. She had inherited millions, and she spent it all endlessly preparing a mansion for the ghosts.

She never finished, she could not have finished since there was no plan, just whatever ideas she had at the time. And she died in 1922, with the mansion not yet "prepared." No ghosts of the rifle dead were ever reported in her lifetime, but now employees of the trust that operates the mansion for tours say that they often see or hear a ghost—the ghost of Sarah Winchester, dressed as she did in life, wandering the mansion still, never finding peace after all.

58 *Helen*

When I moved to California in the early 1970s, I lived with my aunt and uncle just outside Los Angeles in the San Gabriel Valley, right up against the foothills, in a house they had bought recently. After about six months, I was walking back to the house one day and saw a lady kneeling, working in the flower beds—a middle-aged lady with kind of grey hair, wearing a green dress, kneeling at one of my aunt's elaborate flower beds. I didn't think anything about it. I just thought it was someone who worked for my aunt. I didn't mention it.

A couple of weeks later, beside the living room with its open-beamed ceiling and fieldstone fireplace, as I was sitting on the couch in the small den watching television with my uncle, I saw the lady again. She walked by the door to the den and went to the kitchen. She was wearing a black suit-skirt and tailored white blouse with long sleeves. In a few minutes, I got up and went to the kitchen and no one was there. I went to my aunt and asked where the lady that worked for her had gone.

She said, "Tell me what the lady looked like!"

I told her, and she dragged me by the arm back to the den and planted herself in front of the TV. "Ira, listen to me," she said, and then to me, "Tell him who you saw!"

He was very quiet as I told him. He said, "That sounds like Helen."

They told me a strange story.

The former owners were a couple who had quarreled. He shot her in the living room—they showed me the bullet holes in the wall beside the fireplace. Then he burned her body in the huge fireplace and hanged himself from the huge beams in the living room with its cathedral ceiling. No one but my uncle would buy the house because they all feared it. Since my uncle didn't believe the house was haunted, they had never seen her.

I didn't know any better, so I saw her, just as plain as day. Still living in her house, still working in her garden. No one else ever saw her, but from my description they knew who she was. They knew her when she was alive. I didn't meet her until after she was dead.

59 *The Ghost Plays Pool*

We bought and moved into a house that had been owned by a man who never married, and had died of cancer while lying in the living room under the bay window in about 1982. From the day we moved into the house, we had trouble keeping it warm. It was a perfectly nice house, but it had cold spots in it. And it would creak; I always put it to the house settling after the heat of the day. We had put our pool table in the basement, the same room the old owner had loved and used as his rec room, and one he spent a lot of time in, being single. We had the table all leveled, and the kids had been down playing pool one night, and I didn't ever know if they would rack the balls for the next night before they came up, or what. But one night I woke up and heard a ball hit the bottom of a pocket and roll down the return trough to the storage rack.

The table was a weighted one, and it was leveled properly, so the balls weren't rolling into the pockets from gravity or anything. I checked on the kids, and everyone was in bed but me and whoever was playing pool downstairs. It happened once in a while, and I would never go down to see what was happening in the middle of the night. One night I decided to rack the balls and leave them for a game myself, and I watched to see that, in fact, no one went downstairs after I'd done it.

About 2:00 or 3:00 in the morning, I awoke when I heard the balls break. I came up out of my bed...I levitated! And I came down on my feet. My daughter and I, and a nephew staying with us, hit the hall at the same time. We all went to the head of the stairs to the basement, and listened to the balls dropping, one by one, like someone was playing, into the pockets, into the return trough and rolling down into the storage tray.

My daughter said, "Mom, go down there and see what it is."

Well, I didn't go.

I got up early the next morning and went down in the daylight. All the balls I had racked the night before were in the tray. One cue, which I had put in the rack on the wall, was lying catty-cornered across the end of the table.

The answer was simple. When we were through playing, we just left the balls in the tray. The old man had to find some other ghostly entertainment after that.

60 *Yellow with Brown Trim*

Our family bought an old house from a Hispanic family; we moved in the spring, and by fall of that year we noticed that when we got up in the morning, the lights would be on in the kitchen. Then after a while, we noticed one morning that the lights would be on, and the door would be open and the fire would be lit. At first we thought it was something in the electrical wiring that turned the lights on, and we were worried about the house catching fire with an unattended cooking fire, but it was always only in the morning.

We began to be aware of a presence on those mornings, and sometimes the little rocking chair in the corner of the kitchen would be rocking when someone came in, all by itself. We lived there for years and just accepted the fact that someone was getting up early, like a Hispanic mother might, and was getting the kitchen ready for the morning.

We were getting ready to sell the house after a few years, and we decided to repaint before we showed the house. We were deciding what colors to paint the rooms of the house, and someone suggested that we paint the kitchen yellow, with brown trim. All of us thought about it and agreed that that was a good color for the kitchen. We had never lived anywhere with that color combination, and no one knew why we all thought it was such a good idea, but we painted the kitchen yellow with brown trim, and the very next day, the early-morning events came to a stop.

We sold the house a few months later, and the next year we saw the eldest son of the family that we had bought the house from; they had owned the house for generations before us. We told him about the early morning visits to the kitchen, and his eyes got bigger and bigger and bigger. He said that his mother had been a saint; she had been a lovely woman who had raised eight children. She had always been up before everyone else, getting breakfast ready. He said they were always sad that, before she died, they had never given her the one thing she had always wanted.

She had always wished that someday they would paint the kitchen yellow with brown trim.

61   *The Staab House*

The Staab House at La Posada, at 330 East Palace Avenue [in Santa Fe], was the home of the socialite wife of a wealthy German merchant. She furnished her home with the costliest goldware and crystal instead of "laying up her treasures in Heaven" a century ago [in the 1880s]. When she died, she was disconsolate over the loss of her worldly goods. Her spirit still walks the house.

When she comes into the room, a faint cold wind is felt. The candles blow out, and her sobbing is heard as she mourns the loss of her finery and, perhaps, of her immortal soul.

62   *The Fremont House*

In Fremont, California, across from San Francisco, down the coast and out a ways, lived our friends the Browns. He is a computer analyst and she is an executive secretary. They bought a new house, and got a ghost at no extra charge. It's a poltergeist.

He worked nights a lot, and she would lock all the doors while he was away. He would come home to find them unlocked. Hairdryers fell from the cabinets in the bathroom. Canned food moved around in the kitchen and ended up in strange places. The ghost would steal shiny things: keys, tools. Then he'd return them in odd places. They would disappear, things like jewelry, then reappear in plain sight nights later.

They decided his name was Charlie—I don't how they knew that—and that he was a child, or childlike. They'd say out loud, "Now, Charlie…"

I don't really know if I believe that kind of thing or not. But who am I to doubt my friends?

63 *The House on Chalet Road*

Over on Chalet Road, at Lake Taneycomo [Missouri], there is
a haunted house. A man murdered his wife back in the '30s
and buried her body in the cellar. She was from out of state,
and when her family called, he just said she was out of the
house. No one was suspicious for months. When the family
finally came down to find her, they couldn't even find him.
Eventually they suspected the awful truth and dug in the
cellar: there were the remains. The story has been told around
at parties for decades.

Then a close friend named Mike told me his version. He
was at a party in this house—a very nice house, by the
way—and so were, he said, other friends of mine, whom he
named off. Others present that very night agreed they, too,
had been in "that" house on "that" night.

One young lady had gone in to use the toilet, and looked
up to see someone looking in the window. She fled out the
door partially dressed. The guys present ran outside to catch
the "peeper," being very protective of their lady friends, and
found to their shock that the house is built right on the edge
of the cliff above the lake, with a very small passage space
between the house and the steep drop-off. It was pitch dark;
only a fool would walk that narrow way at night. Furthermore, the window to the bathroom was over eight feet up the
outside wall!

There had been people—partygoers—in the front yard,
so no one could have pulled the prank, even if it had been
possible, and gotten away. They asked the girl to describe the
"peeper."

She said it was "an old guy with grey hair." The murderer
had been an old man with grey hair.

Years later, I met a man who started telling me about a
house he had once lived in with some other entertainers I
knew. He said water would come on suddenly. Milk would be
spilled when no one had been in the house. Silverware and
glassware had slid across the counter and fallen to the floor.
He had finally moved out, he said, because one night when
all four 'mates were home with the front door latched, he had
been sitting on his bed taking off his socks. He heard the
screen open and close, and the door open and close, and

footfalls come across the floor toward his bedroom. One of his 'mates came into the room, and said, "My God!" He looked up to see a cloud of smoke evaporate from the air beside him, just outside his peripheral vision. "What was it?" he had asked.

"Didn't you see the man standing next to you?" his friend had said. "He had his hand reached out toward you. It was an older guy with grey hair."

I didn't believe the first story until I heard the second one.

All four guys moved out.

64 El Monte Ghost

My mother lived in El Monte, California, and had a ghost at her house. It wasn't quite a poltergeist; it didn't throw things. What it did was shuffle things around. It was a woman ghost, because it was always in the kitchen, and it took things like beans and macaroni and mixed them together. It would leave the cabinet doors open, too. No matter how often Mother would close the cabinet doors, especially one particular door with the condiments behind it, it would always open.

Sometimes she could even smell the presence of the ghost, because the ghost favored heavy floral, sweet perfume. Up to a point my Father didn't believe there was anyone—or anything—to it. Then one day, he turned to Mother and said, "Did you get enough perfume on?"

She said, "I'm not wearing any perfume. That's the ghost!"

Then he believed her.

Not long after that, my parents moved out and moved away. When they went back to visit old neighbors not too long after that, the neighbor said, "Well, we got your spook. The smell of that perfume is about to drive my wife crazy." The ghost had moved next door when my parents left!

65 Tiny Baby Footprints

Grandmère lived in Kaplan and Crowley [Louisiana] at the time she was growing up. They lived far out of town in an old wooden house with a wood floor. It had a fireplace of fine stonework. In front of the hearth a little distance, so it wouldn't catch a spark, was a country-style braided rag rug.

One night, my cousins told me, there were noises—two particular noises. Something bumped about near the chimneyplace. They also heard a clicking sound they didn't recognize. The dogs began to bark outside. The cousins were so scared that they hid under the covers and didn't get out of bed to see what it was.

In the morning, between the fireplace and the rug, were tiny baby-sized footprints only two or three inches long. The footprints were in the fine ash that had drifted out of the fireplace. It looked as if someone had come down the chimney, scattering ashes as he came, and then left footprints as he walked around the room.

Those footprints are still on that floor today. You can wipe up the ashes, and wipe away the footprints, but they always come back when a new layer of ash settles out on the floor. They're a little fainter now, but you can still see the tiny baby-sized footprints made when there weren't any babies in the family anymore.

66 *Quarai*

Southeast of Albuquerque, in the Manzanos Mountains, stand the ruins of Quarai Mission, which housed missionaries and early Indian Christians. There would have been soldiers there, also, and at least one soldier seems to remain on guard three centuries later.

In the autumn of 1913, visitors to the ruins saw, very late at night, a blue-white light glowing through one of the openings in the ruined adobe walls. In the center of the light stood a Spanish soldier [wearing a tabard emblazoned with a large, red cross whose points ended in *fleurs-de-lys,* the symbol of the military-religious order of Calatrava, and not an uncommon symbol in Spain].

The figure pointed his finger three times and said [most probably], *"Asiste, viador."*

[*Asiste* might mean "attend" or "frequent this place," and *viador* would mean "traveler on a mystic journey." These meanings used in the seventeenth century fit the time period of the mission and of the soldier's uniform, but the message is still unclear.]

67 Horseshoe Ranch

Night voices echo in a barn that was once the headquarters house for the Horseshoe Ranch, outside Tucumcari. Soldiers from old Fort Bascom nearby were escorting a payroll shipment to Fort Sumner in the late 1870s. While they slept in the house, riders, perhaps even hands at the Horseshoe, attacked and killed the soldiers, with only one trooper escaping out the back to bring help.

Reinforcements came, led by the escapee, and the ensuing gunfight killed all the riders. The money was never found; it was not on the bodies of the riders, nor was there any evidence of it having been buried.

Now [as of 1952] the sound of heavy chain and strongboxes being moved about are heard in the cabin at night, along with the faint voices of the riders.

One Quay County resident who didn't believe in the phantoms in the empty cabin spent the night there while trail riding. In the middle of the night, something shoved him out of his bedroll and said, "Move over!"

The man jerked on his boots, jumped on his horse, and moved all the way over to Fort Sumner!

68 Riordan House

I used to work for the Riordan family [in their mansion in Flagstaff, Arizona]. I used to like to sit in the corner seats of the big dining room when my work was done. When I was sixteen, I went to work for the Riordans, and worked...for about five years. This other girl...Henrietta...and I would work here, and we'd stay in the house, or we'd go down to the reservation...on Fridays, I would serve the dinner.

My dad worked for the lumber mill [owned by the Riordans] and I worked here at the house.

They say there's a ghost here in the house...but I don't know...the other gal that used to work with me, she was two years older than me, she was always scared to go by herself to the upstairs, but I told her there's nothing to be scared of. She used to say,

"It seems like I hear the wife...Caroline..she's still here."

After she [Caroline] had died, my youngest brother and my nephew used to come and stay at the house every night...so there would be somebody in the house besides [Mr. Riordan]. My friend, she heard the lady [Caroline] around the house, like when we were doing laundry, and she'd hear her moving around upstairs.

Other Haunted Places

69 El Camino Real

Riders on the old *camino real* [royal road] through Jim Hogg County once met a phantom known as *el blanco* [the white one]. As the rider slowed to pass under branches that overhung the trail, the frightening white spectre would step out of the trees and grab the horse's bridle or reins. The terrified animal might rare up and struggle, but *el blanco* would hold it fast.

One *caballero* [horseman] dared to ask the figure, *"¿Eres de este mundo o del otro?"* [Are you from this world or the next?]

After a moment, the figure answered, *"Del otro."* [From the next world.]

Some horses managed to break away from the grip of *el blanco*. One *caballero* drew his saber and cut the offending hand from the phantom and rode away with the hand still clinging, bloodlessly, to the reins; at sunrise, the hand vanished in a mist.

No one knows what would happen to a rider who did not escape *el blanco*.

No one alive, at least.

70 Palace Hotel

When Cripple Creek, Colorado, was in its glory days as a mining emporium, the palace hotel was lighted by candles. One of the former owners still prefers it that way. Except that she's dead.

The current owners have come into the dining rooms in the dead of winter when the hotel is closed and found candles from the tables lit and often moved to other places than the table on which they belong. The owners say they believe it's the ghost of Mrs. Chambers, who, with her husband, owned the hotel at the turn of the century.

71 White Woman Creek

In Greeley, Wichita, and Scott counties in western Kansas runs the White Woman Creek. There, a peaceful Cheyenne hunting party was attacked by white men, and many Cheyenne were killed. Riding after their attackers, some of the survivors raided the white men's camp and recovered what had been stolen from them. They also took some captives as insurance against further attack.

The prisoners lived with the Cheyenne a year, and when offered their freedom as the Cheyenne moved further west, they decided to stay with the tribe. Several chose husbands or wives among the tribe, and one woman married Tonkawa, a great war chief.

The cavalry attacked the tribe one day in retribution for the taking of prisoners a year before whom the Army assumed to have been killed. Tonkawa was killed, and his bride buried him at the bank of the creek.

She never went back to her own people, and the rest of the Cheyenne moved on west. She wandered the creek until her death, and still wanders the creek at night as a wraith. She sings Indian songs and is heard crying in the wind, wandering along the creek that holds her husband's corpse and bears her name.

72   Old Chief Tawakoni

We [the Austin College football team] used to play Trinity University when the school was located in Waxahachie. We [the Young family] had relatives there, and knew some of the members of the opposing team personally. They told a school spirit story that involved a real spirit.

Old Chief Tawokanny [or Tawakoni] was the ghost of an Indian that walked the hill Trinity had been built on in Tehuacana. He was seen many times in the single old college building or on the campus. Students saw him at night only, and co-eds at the Waxahachie campus were told that he had followed the school to its new location. This absolutely guaranteed the boys a walk home with the girls.

Old Chief Tawokanny was a handy ghost to have around.

73   The Ghost of Rancho de Corrales

Diego Montoya built the hacienda now known as Rancho de Corrales in 1801, but the murderous revenge came after the Emberto family bought the property in 1883. Luis and Luisa Emberto threw elegant parties and dances, but one night the son killed a woman at one of the parties—a woman rumored to be his father's mistress. Luis then moved out and threatened to kill Luisa and her lover, believing that their son had been prompted by his mother in the killing of Lola Griego.

The night of April 30, 1898, Luis returned and shot Luisa as she ran for her own gun. A running gun battle followed, with Luis being killed by José de la Cruz, a one-eyed Indian sharpshooter who was among the posse chasing him.

The manner and circumstances of the Embertos' deaths caused them to be buried on the property, instead of in the *camposanto* [churchyard]. Their graves are somewhere on the opposite side of the irrigation ditch, away from the hacienda, which is now an elegant restaurant. Their ghosts are believed to wander the property even today.

"Have I ever seen the ghosts? Yes and no. I have not seen them, but have felt a pressing sensation here, on the back of my neck, in the old part of the restaurant, which used to be the hacienda itself. Almost everyone who works here feels or sees them sooner or later."

74 Hell and Its Horrors

The Neches River crosses southeast Texas and empties into the Sabine Lake and, by way of the Sabine Pass, into the Gulf of Mexico. The pirate Jean Laffite sailed his ship to the Neches seeking a place to bury some of his vast treasure. Near the river's mouth, his men secured a chain around a sturdy tree and tied off to it. After the treasure was buried, they left the chain in place and sailed back into the gulf.

Over a century later, a Port Arthur man came into possession of a chart left behind when the American Navy ordered Laffite off Galveston Island in 1820. The man followed the chart, found the tree trunk with the chain, and dug at the prescribed place. As he dug, an unseen ghost, perhaps that of Laffite himself, grabbed the man by the throat and began to strangle him. The man fled, leaving his tools behind. He never regained his wits or the power of speech; only by wild gestures could he explain what had happened to him. A week later, he died in his sleep, with his vocal cords and perhaps even his breathing paralyzed, or crushed by the ghost's unseen hand.

A neighbor named Meredith bought the chart and with a partner sought out the chain, the half-dug hole, and the rotting tools. The two began to dig the hole deeper. The pair came to a skeleton, perhaps the hapless pirate who first dug the hole, and was murdered and buried to keep the secret—or to guard the treasure. The bones were gently laid out beside the hole, and the digging continued.

Meredith's partner was in the hole, taking his shift with the spade, when he let out an unearthly scream and jumped from the hole.

Grabbing Meredith, he cried out, "For God's sake, we've got to get out of here!" When Meredith asked what was wrong, the man cried out, "I have seen Hell and its horrors!"

For the second time, the tools were abandoned.

When Meredith dared return much later, and alone, the skeleton was mysteriously back in the hole, but the tools were undisturbed and the hole had not been touched. Solemnly,

Meredith covered the skeleton, and never returned to the treasure grave near the mouth of the Neches.

75 Hell's Half-Acre

There's a place in Arkansas called Hell's Half-Acre. Huge rocks are piled in a sinkhole there, as if something had exploded or torn up the Earth itself. The local folks know: it's the exact place where the Devil is chained, under all those rocks, since he got thrown out of Heaven. When hunters go by, or foolish children play nearby, or tourists come by with their cameras, they hear and smell the most blood-curdling things at sundown or just at dark.

The old Devil under that rock pile cusses something awful, and you can smell his sulphurous hot bad breath floating up out of Hell itself. After all, you're at Hell's Half Acre on Earth!

76 Dance of Death

In the Turkey Mountains of New Mexico, north of Valmora, was Old Fort Union. During the Apache Wars, it was a lonely island of safety in an empty land. A young cavalry lieutenant had fallen in love with the younger sister of his captain's wife. When the troop was ordered out to fight the Apaches, the lieutenant made a grim promise to his beloved.

"No one else will have you, my love. I will return and dance with you again at the wedding, no matter what!"

Weeks later, with no news from the cavalry troop on patrol, the regularly scheduled military ball was taking place at the fort. The young woman attended and received the usual kind attention from all the young officers. During the dance, some of the absent troop returned and reported that many men had been killed and others were missing in action. Among the missing was the lieutenant. The young bride-to-be was much too quickly consoled by another officer, and soon the two were engaged. On the day of the wedding, months later, everyone had gathered for the wedding dance. Before the groom and bride could lead the first dance, in the door strode the missing lieutenant.

His uniform was dirty and bloodstained, but this was not unusual for a man who had been on patrol for months. He was dirty and unarmed, but he did not remove his hat or even greet the crowd. He walked straight to the bride, and bowed as if to dance. Both pleased and saddened to see her former lover, the bride bowed back, and the regimental band struck up a waltz.

The lieutenant danced faster and faster, striking his boots against the floor faster and faster. The band leader followed, and soon the waltz was a thunderous mazurka. The bride seemed to grow faint and pale, but the lieutenant danced on. The woman fainted dead away in his arms, and the dance stopped.

When the lieutenant coldly dropped the bride to the floor, her husband stepped forward and struck the lieutenant, knocking off his hat.

The lieutenant's scalp was gone, and a steel hatchet blade protruded from his open, crushed skull. The grisly figure stood its ground, and slowly faded from human sight, leaving behind only the bride, who was found to be dead.

The following spring, the lieutenant's body was found in a canyon, with a steel hatchet blade embedded in its skull.

77 "Dame, pues, mi asadura"

It was that there was an old widow-woman who lived alone in a small house beside a great pastureland. When her husband had died, she had become very wealthy, and much of the pastureland was hers. Then the cruel *hacendado* [landlord of the hacienda] whose land adjoined hers courted her and persuaded her to sign her land over to him preparatory to their intended nuptials. Like a giddy schoolgirl she signed the parchment. Then his affections grew cool, and her only recompense was a small sum of silver pesos.

Now she sat alone, abandoned, in her little house on her little piece of land, growing older and more bitter with each passing day. One night, having nothing to eat in the house, she decided on a sordid vengeance against the *hacendado*. She would kill one of his prize cattle, slashing its belly to make it look as if the wolves had killed it, leaving the meat to spoil and taking only the innards to make *menudo* [tripe stew].

She wrapped her *rebozo* around her and drew her sharpest knife from the cupboard. Blowing out the candles in her house, she waited at the front door for darkness to fall. As she waited, a funeral procession walked slowly by.

Six men carrying a coffin walked slowly and in step down the road in the gathering darkness. Six old grandmothers dressed in black walked along behind wailing and singing, "*Ay! Qué luto!* [Oh, what sorrow!]" But the widow-woman knew all six of these women, and they were not related to one another. This could only mean one thing: the deceased in the coffin had left money to pay for mourners! Whoever he was, he was alone and unloved.

Then it struck her! She squinted into the gloom and examined the coat of arms on the coffin. It was the *hacendado!* At first she laughed. Then she grew angry. How dare he to die without giving her the chance for revenge?

Then, in her heart, she devised the most horrible revenge.

Wrapping her *rebozo* about her head to conceal all but her eyes, burying the knife deep in the folds of the garment, she joined the procession at the rear. No one took any heed of one more paid mourner. "Oh, what sorrow!" she cried out aloud, but her heart was saying, "*Ay! Desquite!* [Oh, retribution!]"

When the procession reached the holy ground, she stepped aside and stood behind a monument, out of sight. The men laid the coffin into a stone sarcophagus. One of the men passed coins out to the women; he looked for the seventh mourner he had seen, but she was nowhere in sight. He shrugged and pocketed the remaining coins. The old women took their coins, but then spat on the ground, and walked away crossing themselves. The men tried to lift the lid of the sarcophagus, but it was too heavy. They walked away, planning aloud to return the next day with more men.

When all was still and quiet, the widow-woman came out. She walked slowly to the sarcophagus. She bent down and drew out her knife. She pried up the top of the coffin. She reached deep into the dark interior with the knife. She cut out the dead man's entrails to make *menudo. Ay! Desquite!* Back at her house, she put the great black pot on the fire and began to make *menudo.* Soon the pot was boiling. Outside the wind began to blow as if a storm was coming down from the mountains. In the distance, out on the pastureland, the cattle of the dead *hacendado* began to low and call. "Auu," they called, "Auu."

The fire burned bright. The pot boiled high. The wind blew. The cattle called, "A-uura, a-uura." Gradually the call of the cattle seemed to come closer. Gradually it began to seem that the cattle were saying a word: *"Asa'uura, asa'uura...*[Entrails, entrails...]"

The old woman began to become afraid.

Suddenly, she heard the gate of her yard bang open. Was it the wind? Suddenly, she heard footfalls on the pathway to the house, heavy footfalls. Was it the mesquite tree blowing against the wall? Or was it...

The fire blazed. The pot boiled. The wind blew. The cattle called, *"Asadura...Asadura...*Give me back my *asadura...*"

The old woman ran to the door and pulled down the bar. She ran around the house, slamming the shutters and latching them. She ran to the table and cowered beneath it.

Something huge and unimaginably heavy struck the door, knocking once...twice...thrice! Slowly the heavy footfalls began to circle the house, and the wind rattled the shutters one by one, as if someone was trying to get in. The old woman crawled out from under the table and lifted the heavy pot from the hearth. The chimney shook; bits of brick fell into the fire. The old woman struggled to the door, lifted the bar, and set the boiling pot out on the stoop. She slammed the door, pulled down the bar and ran back under the table.

The fire grew low. The wind ceased. The cattle were silent.

After a moment she began to think, "What a silly I am! It was only the wind..."

She crawled out from under the table.

She walked to the door.

She lifted the bar.

She opened...slowly...the door...

Outside, the big black pot was empty.

78 *The Ghost on the Third Floor*

At the music building at Harding College in Searcy, Arkansas, there is a tradition that a ghostly piano player practices by night. From the second floor of the music building, you can hear a piano being played on the floor above you.

According to the story, there were a young man and young woman who were deeply in love, who came from the same town and were both attending Harding at the same time, and both majoring in music. Soon after the school year began, the young man died in an automobile accident. The young woman began to pine and grieve; the only way that she could comfort herself was to go up to one of the private practice rooms on the third floor and play the piano and sometimes sing.

Soon afterwards, she, too, died, apparently from loneliness and grief, before the first semester was even over. Years passed, and people say they still hear her playing on the third floor.

But what makes it mysterious is that since the year she died, the old music building has been torn down, and a new one built in its place. When you stand on the second floor of the new building some nights, you can hear her playing above you...even though the new music building is only two stories tall!

79 The Weeping Lady of Colfax

A friend and I were driving from the Air Force Academy in Colorado Springs, Colorado, to our summer jobs at Philmont in New Mexico, when we left I-25 in Colfax County for a rest stop to get out and stretch. We found ourselves in the town of Colfax, which was a ghost town of burned-out adobe buildings and a large one-room schoolhouse-church with a steeple on top. We climbed around the adobe ruins, and walked up to the schoolhouse.

The frame was fairly solid, and the roof looked dilapidated but intact, but inside the flooring was either rotted away or carried off. Old slate chalkboards and other school and church items were still hanging loosely from the walls. We wondered what might have happened there, how come the people had moved away, and where they had gone. As we left, I could hear a low noise behind us in the schoolhouse, but I didn't think anything of it.

It wasn't until weeks later, at a campfire, that an older ranger who had been away from Philmont for twenty years told a story that gave the visit to Colfax new meaning. He told local tales, and one of them was this:

"A long, long time ago, there was a man and his family living in Colfax. His favorite son grew ill and died at the tender age of ten, at the turn of the century. The boy had attended the one-room school, but that building was also the church, so the funeral was held there too. The mother sat in the back during the service and wept and wailed with uncontrollable grief.

"For weeks after, day in and day out, the grieving mother would go to the school and sit in the back on a bench and mourn and cry.

"She was so sad and morose that she just pined away, and within a month, she also passed away. The dozen or so families of the community held services for her in the schoolhouse-church, and she, too, was buried, beside her son, in the graveyard.

"In the months ahead, every Sunday, in the evening or at night, the ghost of the grieving mother would reappear in the back row of benches at the church, wailing and weeping. She became know as the Weeping Lady of Colfax.

"The sight and above all the sound of the Weeping Lady was so unnerving that one by one the families moved away and abandoned the schoolhouse, and the sight of the Weeping Lady so alarmed drifters and other passers-by who sought refuge in the structure that someone tore out the flooring to discourage visitors from staying at dusk.

"Since Colfax was halfway between Cimarron and Raton, wagons often stopped at Colfax for water or rest, and many travellers who reached Raton told of seeing the Weeping Lady. Many of those who saw her never knew she was a ghost, she looked and sounded so real."

Then I knew why the floorboards were gone..and what I had heard in the old schoolhouse-church at Colfax.

80 *The Devil's Neck*

From the road here in Placitas, looking to the west, over by Mount Taylor, you can see the *Cabezón*. The story goes that this mesa is the Devil's Neck. When young Spanish soldiers came from over the sea to the New World, many of them were only teenagers. One young man was only fourteen when he left Cadiz; he took his sword which his grandfather had given him and had it blessed by the bishop at Madrid and had its double edge sharpened anew. He brought the sword across the sea to Mexico and north to El Paso, and he was among the few chosen to come northward seeking the Lost Cities of Gold.

The young hero's troop came up to Zuni Pueblo, and then to Zia Pueblo, and then attempted to travel northward to Taos. They wandered off course somewhat and encamped on the farthest northern reaches of Mount Taylor at a spring where they could spend two or three days and rest the horses. The last night at the spring, it was the young hero's stand at watch. The fire burned low and all the men were snoring, and the young man fell asleep, a mortal sin for a sentinel.

He awoke with a hot wind blowing against the side of his face, even though it was spring and shortly before dawn, when it should have been the coolest time of the day. It was not a desert breeze, it was a harsh, hot wind. He stood and turned to face this hot wind, and he saw the Devil's head, as large as a mountain, staring at him and breathing down on him. The Devil's mouth opened and his red-hot tongue unrolled toward all the sleeping soldiers.

Since he was the sentinel, and it was his duty to protect them, he responded with all the courage and fortitude that he had, knowing that his grandfather and everyone at home had believed in him. He drew his great, double-edged sword from its scabbard and swung it with all his strength. With the first blow, he cut open the front part of the Devil's neck. As he swung the sword back, he finished severing the huge head from the spinal cord of the Devil. The grotesque head rolled back, behind the Devil's neck and shoulders, back down into the Underworld, with a horrible, horrible scream that woke everyone up. The Devil's neck and shoulders slowly lowered back into the Underworld, and everyone stood and praised the little hero with the great sword.

And now, every morning, if you go up in the high mountains, and you look to the west, here, you see the Devil's shoulders and the Devil's neck, rising up in the west, and he waits all day for the boy to come back and put the head on its rightful place. That is the story of *el Cabezón* [the Great Head].

81 The Devil's Breath

Settlers came westward and went up on *Cabezón,* knowing that the Indians would not disturb them there, because the Indians did not like that place. These pioneers thought that the high vantage of *Cabezón* would be a good place to sit and look out on the valley. They built a village there, with farms and schools, on the flat top of *Cabezón,* the Devil's Neck.

The only contact these settlers had with the world in the valley below them was a circuit priest who came up every six months to hold marriages, baptisms, and hear confession. And to bury the dead. On his first visit, the priest took a census. A flood in the valley prevented him from returning his next appointed time, but at the end of one year, when he returned to the mesa top, he found all the people dead.

The people had fallen over wherever they stood. One man lay dead in the field, still holding his plow tied to a dead ox. One woman fell over churning butter, and overturned her churn. The children in the schoolyard lay dead at their games. The priest thought that the people had turned to sin and lost their Holy Spirit, and evil had come and taken them away.

The priest brought a company of men from the valley below to bury the dead and bring the possessions down to sell them off in Bernalillo and Santa Fe and Cuba. Everyone who knew the story of how *el Cabezón* came to be knew that the people had died from the hot sulphurous breath coming out of the Devil's Neck.

Later in the 1950s, some squatters went back up there to try to live, but the people were getting ill from the spring water. The EPA [Environmental Protection Agency] went up there and found that the spring waters were full of strychnine [or poisonous alkaloids]. Nobody lives up there now.

82 The Ghost of Ella Barham

It seems that ghosts most often walk in the place where they were murdered. They most often haunt a place where they died by violence, or mutilation, or without warning. Fox hunters and 'coon hunters along Crooked Creek near the Killebrew Ford, about eighteen miles below Harrison [Arkansas], say they still see the ghost of Ella Barham, dressed all in white, walking near the mine shaft where her body was found.

On November 21, 1912, Ella was out riding; her horse came back without her. That night, hunters spotted a herd of hogs loudly rooting around some suspicious looking objects under a loose pile of rocks near an abandoned mine shaft. It was a corpse, cut into pieces by a saw. There were signs the body had been carried over the Crooked by the murderer, who must have surprised her on the road, to be disposed of.

Even though he joined in the search for the girl before her body was found, a young man named Odus Davidson was suspected of the crime. A local justice of the peace was of the opinion that Odus had been jilted by Ella not long before. The day afterward, the local judge swore out a warrant for Odus's arrest. At his family's house, when the posse came to get him, Odus jumped out a back window and fled to the woods. He had peppered his socks to keep bloodhounds from trailing him, but he was taken without resistance and admitted to having been cutting wood near the place Ella had last been seen. He had come through my yard not long after that time of day.

The flight, the peppered socks, the presumed jilting, the admission of being near the death scene, and the blood on his socks when he was caught were enough to sway the jury for conviction. We deliberated a short time and returned a guilty verdict. Odus Davidson was hanged just before the Arkansas death penalty was changed to electrocution at the state penitentiary's death house. Odus Davidson was the last man hanged legally in Arkansas.

The body of the victim had been cut up horribly, into seven pieces, but the ghost the hunters claim they see down on Crooked Creek is all in one piece. The prosecutor at the trial had quoted Bible verses, turned to Odus shouting," And where is Ella Barham?"

I guess the answer could be, "Still down at Crooked Creek, near Pleasant Ridge."

83 *White River Boy*

In the 1920s, White River [Arizona] Apache Reservation had a Lutheran Mission, with an assistant rector whose wife had

had a child. The boy seemed fine until he reached the age of walking and talking, but he didn't do any of the latter; he was probably autistic, but they didn't have a word for it then. He was a beautiful child, and he walked and ran and played, but he never spoke. He was dark, with the most beautiful eyes, almost yellow, and had the most intelligent look, as if he were trying to get through to you but couldn't.

He constantly tried to get away, as if he didn't belong in the house. He had a sandbox to play in, and they had built a high fence to keep him from climbing out and running away. They had to watch him constantly. One day the mother left him alone in the sandbox for just a moment while she stepped inside; when she came back, he was gone. He had climbed the fence and headed for the river.

They found him later, drowned.

None of the Anglo people ever saw it, but the Apaches said they saw the boy for years thereafter, walking along the river. It was as if he were a visitor from another world who wanted to go back where he came from.

84 *Cousin Jack and the Buccas*

"Cousin Jack" came from Cornwall [England] to mine the Comstock Lode in Nevada in the 1880s. Hiding in his knapsack was a *bucca,* a Cornish hobgoblin, who had come from the deep mines in Southwestern England. The *buccas* prospered more than the miners did, and soon every deep mine had one or two living in its walls. When Cousin Jack ate his pasties at lunch, he always left a bite behind in the shaft for the *buccas.* Bad luck came for sure if he neglected his imp-friends: his tools got misplaced, his lamp went out suddenly, or gravel fell in his lunchpail. But if he fed the little beasties, they would tap inside the walls and warn him in time of an impending cave-in. Englishmen claimed the ghosts of dead miners haunted the mines and tapped: Cornishmen knew it was the *buccas.*

85 *Wailing Women of Katzimo*

The Acoma people used to live on Katzimo, the Enchanted Mesa, over there [near Acoma Mesa]. The crops were good and life was so easy the people forgot to do the dances to pray to the gods, and they did not teach their children properly. One day three old women who were ill stayed in the pueblo while all the others were in the fields on the valley floor below. Only a young boy was left with them to see to their needs.

The Great Thunderbird came over the mesa and showed the gods' displeasure by shaking his wings and bringing great rain. The rain was so great that the pueblo was falling apart; the mud and rocks were giving away. The women sent the boy to go down to the fields and bring the men back, even in this storm, to the pueblo. As the boy was climbing down the rock-face ladder, one part of the cliff fell away, the part with the handholds cut in it.

No one could get back up to the pueblo. The old women looked down and saw the people, but they couldn't get down. They starved up there, punished for the pueblo's not teaching the children properly. In the winter, at night when the wind blows, you can still hear those old women wailing on Katzimo, the Enchanted Mesa.

86 *Dead Man's Curve*

It was a long time ago, at Dead Man's Curve, between Paradis and Des Allemands [in St. Charles parish, Louisiana] on an old road that runs along the railroad track. There was a little cemetery where the relatives set out voudou regalia on the graves. My friends and I used to run through and pick up black candles to use in séances when we were in high school. The road goes on past the cemetery to a real sharp curve that they call Dead Man's Curve. In the forties or fifties, before—I think—the road was paved, a young couple in a roadster took the curve too fast and were killed. I heard it said that they had sped away when they saw something in the cemetery.

If you slow down or stop after midnight at the curve, you can hear them scream, and you see these pillars of blue light moving among the trees. There's a "swamp phosphorous" that glows, that is used as the explanation for this, but that's ridiculous. We drove through slow one night and stopped because we heard the screams; we watched. These lights were moving. Now, swamp phosphorous doesn't move. These lights move, big pillars of blue light, taller than a person, coming toward the road, then turning and "walking" back off into the woods. Needless to say, we left—very quickly.

I've heard this story over and over, but I saw this! We heard, like, tires screeching, then a boy's voice screaming, then we saw the lights. Then we left!

87 The Presence at the Lodge

In the early '70s, my husband and I were "into" yoga, and we went to an old, converted hot-springs resort in northern California where a yoga group ran a yoga retreat guided by a swami. The resort was built in the '20s, with individual cabins as well as the main lodge. There were also the hot baths, with hot mineral water, in another building. About twenty people were staying there.

The unmarried men were in one dormitory, and the unmarried women in another, and the married couples lived in the cabins. We weren't encouraged to talk with others; we did our chores and studied, meditated, or whatever you were doing. So, there wasn't a lot of conversation, and I did not hear any "warning" of what was to come.

My husband was away for the weekend, and at night—I had no clock or watch so I don't know what time of night it was—all of a sudden, an energy mass appeared before me and was pulsating toward me. I was terrified. It was not a shape of a human being, it was just a pulsing mass. I don't know if I visually saw it or sensed it; it was dark and I was not aware of a color. The energy was definitely feminine, I felt, and hostile.

It is customary for a student of yoga to progress along her spiritual path, and at some point to confront interference. At this point, she would go for a meeting with the swami, or the head of the retreat, for planning the future path to follow. I thought that I was sensing interference, but it was not a happy presence, and it frightened me. I was not prepared, however, for what he told me.

Yes, he said, this is an old place, and there are spirits still lingering here. Every married woman who had been left alone for a time since the first retreat several years before had experienced and reported this same thing. They had—every single one of them—felt something was in the room with them, and felt threatened. The presence had not been discussed individually among the retreat participants; its existence had come out in a group meeting after married women had reported it. The single women were not a virgin community, but then again, they were seldom alone in their dormitory.

The head teacher explained the presence by saying that there are beings that are not ready to leave and, lacking bodies, try to relive their existence through whatever live beings are present. I left a light on all the time until my husband returned, and never felt her presence again.

88 The Lady of the Ledge

In Old Oraibi, on the Hopi Land, where no non-Indian is allowed to go, there sits a black ravine known as Coal Canyon. On nights when the moon is full, from the canyon floor looking up, you can see her dancing on the rim: The Lady of the Ledge.

She was once an old woman, insane, wandering the endless canyons and mesas. She walked off the edge one day, ending her life of her own will. That is not the Hopi way: she was not accepted into the Other World. She returns to This World on nights the moon is full, dancing on the ledge, slow and white in the full moonlight, dancing on the ledge.

Some people who have seen her suspect that she is an optical illusion caused by the shimmer of heat rising off the rock wall as the cool of evening comes to the desert. But I have seen her, and she is dancing. She is The Lady of the Ledge.

89 Rancho de las Chimeneas

In Maverick County [Texas], you'll find *Rancho de las Chimeneas:* Chimney Ranch. On the property, far off the beaten path, stands the ruin of the old stone hacienda from

Spanish Colonial days. Sometimes a lone rider or a fence-repair gang would sleep in the old house, with a fire in one of its many chimneys, one in almost every room.

One night a group of cowpokes slept in the house. In the darkest part of the night, they awoke to hear heavy footfalls on the dirt floor and the jingling of old-fashioned, large-roweled spurs, like the Spanish used to wear. The spurs got closer and closer until one cowboy, a Mexican, let out a scream of fear and managed to light a match. No one was there but the bootless men in their sleeping bags.

The *vaquero* was so scared, he got the *susto* [dread], and the *curandero* had to clear his mind of evil spirits by sweeping him with a broom.

90   The Exchange House Well

In La Fonda, the inn at the plaza in Santa Fe, there is a distraught gambler who dies over and over again. When the hotel was called The Exchange House and gambling was legal, a travelling salesman lost in a card game all his own money and all the money entrusted to him by his company's home office. In despair, he expiated his shame by jumping into the hotel's water supply, a well, and drowning.

The dining room called La Plazuela is located over the site of the old well, long since covered. Diners there sometimes see the ghostly form walk to the middle of the room and jump into the floor and vanish down the no-longer-visible well. His expiation was incomplete and goes on over and over again.

91   The Lookout Rider

According to local legend, there was a Confederate lookout post on Inspiration Point [the highest point along the ridge road west of Branson, Missouri]. A lone rider could spot any kind of large troop movement and take the word to nearby encampments. On that site today is a theme park honoring "The Shepherd of the Hills," the novel by Harold Bell Wright. In a nighttime pageant—which involves a ghost as a character, by the way—actors on horseback move in and out of the woods as part of their roles.

Every once in a while, there's one horseman too many.

In about 1964, a panther was bothering the horses kept on the park for trail rides and the nighttime play. Some of the local folks claimed it was a booger cat, not a real cat at all. All the employees were especially watchful around that time, keeping an eye out for a panther. This increased state of watchfulness led to them seeing something else, or someone else: a horseman who did not resemble any of the employees, on a horse that no one recognized, riding the trails at night.

Some of the actors, the best horsemen, chased the rider at night and could never catch him, almost as if he weren't human- and horse-flesh. It may all be a scary story told around campfires, and not true at all, but at least one actor swears it's true, and that he knows who it is: a Confederate sentinel, fleeing the actors dressed as Baldknobbers, a post–Civil War vigilante group that was pro–Union!

92 *Unseen Hands*

...[T]wo men were prowling around in the Baltimore Mine...for the purpose of seeing whether there was ore enough in sight to extract profitably on tribute. Climbing into a stope, they heard the click of hammers and were very much surprised...to see two striking hammers hard at work on the head of a rusty drill which was being deftly turned by unseen hands, and though not a soul was in sight except themselves, they heard a lively conversation; they could make out no words. They looked and listened for some minutes, until fear took hold and drove them out of the mine quickly.

At the Toll House, they related their experience and were laughed at, but to prove that their heads were clear, they conducted a couple of skeptics to the spot and found the hammer still at work.

[Extract from the Virginia City, Nevada, *Chronicle,* October 8, 1884.]

93 *The Statue That Moves*

In Southwest City, Missouri, there is a graveyard with a statue that moves, a very frightening statue that moves. There is a woman carved in stone on top of a headstone. I myself have seen this happen: sometimes you will look at the statue and it's kneeling with its hands clasped in front of it, with its head bowed. Other times, the head is up and the arms are lowered. The statue changes position from time to time.

94   *Great-Uncle Pius's Gold*

Great-Uncle Pius buried his gold during the Civil War because he had heard that the Union Army was coming toward his home. He buried it at the foot of a tree in one of his pastures, where his big white bull kept everyone out. Pius died in the war, and ever since, the family has looked for this gold.

Two separate fortune-tellers have said that the treasure is guarded by something white. These were *traiteures* [people who heal by prayer and the laying-on of hands] whom the family had consulted. They didn't know about the white bull. He died a long time ago, too, but he must still be guarding the treasure as a ghost.

The family would drive iron rods into the ground trying to strike the chest. They never found it, so the ghost must be doing a good job.

95   *Superstition Mountain*

Along the southern belt of the country, from the Carolinas to California, from the Cherokees in the east to the Apaches in the west, the Indian People tell about the Little People. Little People are about three or four feet tall, and they are associated with sun-worship.

One tribe of Little People lived in the Superstition Mountains. With them lived a woman with golden hair who was a special friend of the Sun. The neighboring Zunis coveted the golden-haired woman and attacked the Little People to take her captive. The Zunis said that they had brought the golden-haired woman from the place of the rising sun, and she belonged to them.

When the Zunis approached the village of the Little People, the golden-haired woman came out and confronted them. She carried a clay pot and poured its contents out into the Salt River. The pot was full of fire and sparks of the sun. Sparks jumped from the river and bounced off the rocks. Balls of fire rolled down the river and drove the Zunis away.

The Little People went and hid in a cave near the Salt River, and the Apaches came and tried to take the golden sun-woman. Again, she rolled balls of fire and sparks at the Apaches, and they were driven away.

The Apaches say that the Little People are still hiding in a cave in the Superstition Mountains, and it is they who have made so many miners and prospectors disappear. The sparks and balls of fire are still sometimes seen in the Superstitions today.

Supernatural and Preternatural
(Including the Miraculous, the Devil, Death, Monsters, Witches, and Such)

96 *The Specter of Death*

As most of you know [the teller nods toward a newcomer in a circle of friends gathered for ghost-story telling], I run the one-hour photo in the mall. About four years ago [1985], a man with a whole roll of negatives already developed came in and wanted some prints made while he waited. I ran the film through, but the pictures were so dark, I wasn't getting a decent print. We did finally get one negative to print out where you could barely see the image. I told him I might get a better print if I knew what I was looking for. Here's the print [he produces a dim color print and passes it around], and here's what the guy told me:

Quite a while ago, four men went on a hunting trip in Colorado. They had been told that the spot they'd picked to camp in was a valley that strange things had happened in before, but they camped there anyway, because they didn't believe it. The first two nights, they heard strange sounds on the wind, but the third day they went out to hunt, and as they came back to camp at sundown, they saw this! [He refers to the photo, and describes it.]

That's a four-man tent, there, and it's seven feet tall. You can see standing beside it is a figure dressed in black, about ten or eleven feet tall. He looks just like the figure of death. [Those present examine the photo. It does, indeed, seem to be what he is describing.] They had one camera with them, an old one-twenty-six, that's why the picture's square; they shot about two-thirds of the roll of this thing. That's the only picture that came out on the whole roll, the rest of them were just about black. They abandoned their equipment and walked or ran out right then, and never went back.

Within two years, I was told, one died accidentally, one died under mysterious circumstances, one guy committed suicide, and the last one, who shot this picture, had been in an asylum for many, many years. The man who brought me the photos is a researcher from California who had heard about this and finally came all the way here to talk to the only person still alive who witnessed this.

From there, he got a-hold of a relative and had to dig through all his negatives to find this one roll, and, as I said, that's the only picture on the roll that came out. He wanted that one picture badly enough that we worked with him for about two hours getting it. We ran several prints, and he took the best ones, and I put this one in a drawer at the shop, and it's been there until tonight.

You can have that one, by the way.

97 The Fouke Monster

My grandfather took a shot at the Fouke Monster. Not many folks have ever done that. The thing was seen many times, usually at dusk, always near the riverbed or the creeks, usually along Boggy Creek where it crosses U.S. Highway 71.

The Fouke Monster is best remembered by those who heard its roar. Some people said it was like a panther scream-ing, but most said it was unlike anything they'd ever heard before. Those who said they'd seen it said it was as tall as a man, hairy like an ape, and walked upright. It had a foul smell that hunting dogs wouldn't track, and some people claimed it left three-toed tracks in the field mud.

The monster was reported on the national news after it terrorized two families sharing a house near Boggy Creek. The sheriff came from Texarkana and reported finding panther tracks, but the believers around Fouke were sure it had been the monster.

Later, they made a movie about it, and my grandfather played himself in it. The thing was messing around his chicken pens.

The monster was blamed for killing hogs or stealing chickens, and most of all, for the unexplained deaths of hunting dogs; torn and broken carcasses were found in yards or fields or woods. Dogs were scared of the thing; they howled when it came near.

The dogs were howling at my grandfather's place around dusk one day, and he loaded his shotgun. The squawking from the henhouse told him what was happening. From the back porch, he fired into the dark shadows in the chicken-yard. The thing fled noisily through the underbrush. He never saw it clearly.

I think he preferred it that way.

98 *Death and the Curandero*

There was an old man who killed a chicken and was cooking it over a fire. St. Peter came along and asked for a bite. The poor man said, "No, blessed Saint Peter, for you neglect the poor. The rich have so much, and the poor have so little. You do not treat us all equally."

Saint Peter went away without saying anything.

Then along came Saint Anthony and asked for a bite. The poor man said, "No, blessed Saint Anthony, for your bishops neglect the poor. The poor box [in the cathedral] is very small and the offering basket is very large. You do not treat us equally."

Saint Anthony went away with a sigh.

Then along came Death herself and asked for a bite. "Yes, Sister Death," said the poor man, "I'll give you a bite, for you take the souls of the rich and the poor. You don't play favorites. You treat us all equally." And he gave her a chicken leg, which she ate.

"I will give you a *merced* [boon]," said Death. "What do you wish?"

"Give me what you will," said the poor man, "and I'll be glad to get it."

"I will give you the *merced* of being a *curandero* [folk healer; herbal healer]," she said. "And when you come to cure someone, you must look and see where I am standing. If I stand at the head of the sick man's bed, he is doomed and you will not be able to cure him. If I stand at the foot, you may heal him. But never, never try to heal the ill person if I stand at the head of the bed."

And she went away.

The man became a *curandero* and grew wealthy giving out herbal remedies and teas, chanting over the sick, and blowing away the bad airs from the sick. Each time, if he saw Death at the head of the sick person's bed, he said, "This one is beyond help, only call a priest and pay me nothing."

Then one night he was called to the bedside of a very rich old man. There stood Death at the head of the bed. "This one is beyond help," said the *curandero,* but the old woman said, "I will pay you a thousand silver pesos to cure him." The *curandero* found he could not finish his sentence.

He took out his medicines and began to chant and gyrate in a loud silly way, and he circled the bed, and he shoved Death around to the foot of the bed in the process. Then he healed the man by his normal means and took the thousand silver pesos home. He put the money in a bag for safekeeping and placed it under his pillow and went to sleep.

During the night he awoke and turned to look at his money under the pillow. In the moonlight, there was Death, at the head of the bed. He was found the next morning, with his cold dead fingers around the money bag.

99 *Pedro de Urdemalas*

Then there's the story of Pedro de Urdemalas (Tricky Pete) the *pícaro* [young vagabond who lives by his wits] who tricked Old Mister Death and his wife and children. Pedro earned his living as a beggar, and one day as he whistled and walked along the road, a beggar asked him for alms!

"You must be very poor indeed," said Pedro, "to beg from a beggar!"

Pedro gave the beggar all the coins in his pocket, and the beggar said. "Now, you may ask me for something in return."

"Very well," said Pedro, thinking it was a playful chatter just to pass the time, as beggars often did. "Give me a magical deck of playing cards wherewith I always win, and no one can quit playing unless I say so."

"Done," said the beggar.

"Give me a flute-and-drum," said Pedro, "that, once begun, no one can quit playing until I am tired of dancing and say so."

"Done," said the beggar.

"Give me a dense greasewood thicket [creosote bush; *Larrea mexicana*] wherein I can throw those to whom I owe money, and they can't get out until I say so."

"Done," said the beggar, "but shouldn't you forsake these vain and worldly things and concern yourself with your soul?"

"Very well," Pedro sighed. "Let it be that when I knock on the Doors to Heaven, St. Peter will let me in, no matter what."

"That's more like it," said the beggar, and he stood up. His dirty robe became white, and the keys to the Kingdom hung at his belt. St. Peter went away and left behind the things Pedro had requested.

Pedro gambled a lot and always won. He danced a lot and never paid the piper. And he threw a lot of creditors into the greasewood until they forgave his debts to them. Finally, it came time for Pedro to die.

Little Death [one of the children of Old Man Death, an Aztec concept] came along and claimed Pedro's soul to take it to Hell. "Very well," said Pedro, "but let's play some cards first." Little Death agreed, and couldn't stop playing. Soon, those predestined to have died were walking all about and Little Death begged to be set free to go about his business. Pedro let him go on condition that he allow Pedro to live twice as long. He agreed.

Finally, the day came for Pedro to die, and Old Lady Death came for him. "Before I go," said Pedro, "let me give all my worldly goods to the poor." Old Lady Death agreed. "Here," said Pedro as he gathered up belongings, "you carry the drum." Old Lady Death took up the flute-and-drum and was soon playing them and couldn't quit. Pedro went away for seven days. When he got back, Old Lady Death begged to be set free to go about her business. Pedro let her go, on condition that she let him live twice as long. She agreed.

Finally, the day came for Pedro to die. Old Man Death himself came for Pedro. "I'll go peacefully," said Pedro, "wait here by this greasewood bush." Pedro tried to throw Old Man Death into the greasewood bush, but the Old Man was too smart for him. He broke off a thorny switch and chased Pedro down the road to Hell.

Pedro ran around and around in circles until Old Man Death was dizzy, and then he ran up the road toward Heaven. When got to the doors of Heaven, with Death right behind him, he knocked, and St. Peter came to answer the door.

"Where have you been?" said St. Peter angrily.

"I've been busy," said Pedro. "Let me in as you promised me!"

St. Peter let him in, and Old Man Death crushed the greasewood switch until it bled grease and burst into flames. And that's the story of Pedro de Urdemalas.

100 *The Flying Head*

Once there was a great Flying Head. It was so huge that it was as big as a lodgehouse. It had great big eyes, as big as wagon wheels; it had great big wings growing out of its sides where its ears might have been; it had a big wide mouth with hundreds of teeth like the points of double-edged knives. But its nose was a little-bitty nose no bigger than a child's.

When the Flying Head was hungry, it flew through the skies grinding its teeth together—*gnash, gnash, gnash!* It flew through the skies beating its wings—*whoosh, whoosh, whoosh!* The Head would fly over a pueblo and swoop down, eating whole herds of pigs or goats or carrying off a cow or a burro or even a person! When the People heard the Flying Head coming, they would hide under the floorboards of their houses. The Head only came out at sunrise or sunset, so the People were safe if they went out in the heat of the day.

There was a young mother in one pueblo who could only let her baby outside in the hottest part of the day, and she was sad that her child only saw the sun high in the sky. She wanted to be able to go out in the cool of the morning and the beauty of the evening. She decided to do something about it!

One day near dusk, when the People expected the Head might come, the young mother took her baby to a neighbor and asked her to watch the child for a while. Then she went to another neighbor and asked for some firewood, which he gave her. She took the wood to her house and built a fire. Then she went down by the river and picked up a basketful of round, smooth stones. She put the stones on the hearth, and slowly pushed them into the fire with a stick.

Soon the Flying Head was coming! *Whoosh, whoosh, whoosh,* went the wings in the sky; *gnash, gnash, gnash* went the teeth in its mouth.

The young mother heard the sound coming. She took a wooden spoon and lifted the red-hot stones out of the coals. One by one she put them in a bread bowl. She put the bread bowl on the table. Outside she heard the People calling out from house to house, telling everyone to hide under the floorboards. But she sat at the table, and did not look to either side.

The Head flew into the pueblo and swooped about, looking into the houses. The young mother said loudly, "Good bread...good hot bread," and she lifted a hot stone towards her mouth. Then, at the last moment, she dropped the stone into the sand beside the hearth. The Flying Head flew over and looked in the window of the house; he flew back and forth, looking in first with one big eye and then the other.

"Good bread," said the young mother, "good hot bread." And she lifted another hot stone towards her open mouth, dropping it into the sand when the Head was between eyes at the window. She rubbed her stomach and smacked her lips. The Head put its little nose in the window, but it couldn't smell any bread. *Sniff, sniff, sniff,* went the Head. The young mother didn't look to either side.

"Good bread," she said, lifting another hot stone, "good hot bread." The Head was at the doorway, looking in. She passed the stone by her open mouth and dropped it over her shoulder into the sand. She rubbed her stomach again.

The Flying Head reached its wings into the doorway and took the bread bowl off the table. The Head tipped up the bowl and swallowed all the hot rocks. The frightened young mother didn't look to either side; she sat still and looked straight ahead.

The Head dropped the bowl and began to beat its wings. It flew up in the sky and flew around and around, blowing smoke out its mouth. The Head flew way, way up into the sky and burst into a thousand, thousand pieces, and never bothered the People again. The young mother went and told the neighbors what had happened, and thanked them, and brought her baby home. And after that, she and her baby sat in the plaza in the morning and in the evening, any day they wanted.

101a *The Lady in Blue I*

The great Father Alonso de Benavides came to the upper Rio Grande valley in New Mexico in 1629. When he arrived, he found that the Jumano Indians were already asking for missionaries instead of rejecting them as other tribes did. When asked why they were so blessedly eager and how they had known of the Christian missionaries, they told a strange and miraculous story.

A European woman with light skin, dressed in a blue robe from neck to feet, came among the Jumanos for many years, for many generations teaching them in their own tongue and promising missionaries would come to them in the future. As far away as Texas, the Blue Lady was seen for years before the arrival of the missionaries.

The Blue Lady was very beautiful and kind, and spoke all the Indian languages.

One woman from Spain said that she had been the Blue Lady, and that she had been transported miraculously to the New World for the visits, but this explanation seems inadequate, for the Blue Lady was seen before this woman was even born back in Spain. The Franciscans of the seventeenth century believed that the Blue Lady was even more supernatural than miraculous transport: they believed she was a visitor from the Other World.

101b *The Lady in Blue II*

In the Pueblo, they used to tell the story of how in Agreda, Spain, there lived a beautiful girl named María Coronal de Agreda. She was born in 1602 and she died in 1665. As the story goes, this young woman, who had heard tales of the New World and the Indians, spent a lot of her time praying for the conversion of the Indians, who at that time knew little of God. It so happened that around this time, she was offered a trip to go to New Spain.

After her very long journey, illness, and prayer, she found herself among the Indians that were unheard of in Europe. She could not stay long because of her health, and she had to return. But she promised that she would send teachers to help the Indians who also suffered from illnesses.

In the 1680s, a missionary named Damián de Manzanet discovered in New Mexico the Indians written about in the writings of María Coronal de Agreda. They joyfully received Manzanet, and one day the chief asked Manzanet for some blue baize to bury his grandmother in, for she had recently died. Manzanet asked why he wanted such a strange color of cloth. No Europeans wearing blue were there.

The Indian replied that it was because he had once seen a beautiful woman who had come to help them and whom they honored in their stories, and who wore blue. The chief said he wished to be like the Blue Lady and pass into Heaven, where his spirit could be at peace.

But María de Agreda had never gotten as far north as New Mexico, and yet the Tanoan [language group of] Indians remember her in legend and tell that where she walked, her footsteps had caused wild blue flowers to bloom.

102 *The Disobedient Granddaughter*

It happened that there was a lovely young girl from El Paso del Norte who had come to her fifteenth spring and wanted to go out into the world and dance with young men. Her old grandmother with whom she lived disapproved, however, and forbade her to go to the parties that season. One night she slipped out a window with a loose grill and went to the dance anyway.

At the dance, she met a handsome young man with dark flashing eyes and a gracious manner. They danced and danced almost until dawn. He asked her to run away with him and be his bride. The foolish young girl was infatuated with the handsome man, and she agreed to elope. As she climbed back in through the loose grill, she told him to wait.

As he waited, he paced back and forth, and then he sat down for a moment to remove his boots, which were hurting his feet. As he paced back and forth under the window, he left footprints.

Rooster footprints.

When the young woman came back with her portman-teau, the young man had his boots on, but she saw the huge rooster tracks in the dirt. Realizing the young man was the Devil in disguise, she opened her bag and pulled out her crucifix, which she had packed.

When the Devil saw the crucifix, he ran away and never came back. And the young woman never again disobeyed her old grandmother.

103 *The Wolf Girl of Devil's River*

Hunters from all over Texas go to San Angelo to hunt south of there in Crockett and Val Verde counties. On the Devil's River, which flows out of Buckhorn Draw to the *Río Bravo del Norte,* called in Texas the Rio Grande, hunters watch for many kinds of game. And one kind of ghost.

Texas' most famous ghost is the Wolf Girl of Devil's River, seen as a feral child in the 1800s and as a white phantom until recently. No one really wants to see the Wolf Girl, who is variously described as a white shape, a naked woman, or an albino wolf.

Settlers in the territory west of San Antonio in the early 1800s were prey to many dangers, including unfriendly In-dians and Mexican *bandidos.* A couple with a baby was mur-dered and the baby left to die. Passersby found the bodies of the couple, but the baby was gone. Wolf tracks seemed to indicate the baby's fate. For years afterward, a wild child was sighted roaming with the wolves. Some ranchers claimed to have captured the girl, only to have her escape with the help of a pack of howling wolves. She was seen again in 1852, and 1875. A wolf might live fifteen years, a woman might live seventy, but the Wolf Girl was seen for over a century and a half.

Very few people see the Wolf Girl, and fewer admit to it. But she is still seen, as recent books testify in reports by hunters who ask to remain anonymous. She's Pecos Bill's spiritual cousin, and may even be the origin of that coyote-raised boy's legend.

If you hear the call of a canine at night along the Devil's River, it may not be a dog. It may not be a coyote. It may not even be a wolf.

If the cry sounds neither human nor animal, that may be exactly what it is!

104 *The Hairy Man*

In Central Texas, where I used to live, people talk about a hairy man who lives in the woods. I didn't ever believe in him until two years ago. My mother and I were living alone together in a rundown house near a creek bed. We...didn't have any money, and so the place only had a well and an outhouse. It was my job to go out and get a bucketful of water when Mother needed it.

One morning real early, I got up and there was a fog on the creek bottom. I couldn't see but a few feet in front of me. It was cold and wet, but I had to have water, and Mother wasn't up yet because she slept late on Saturdays. And usually, I did too, except this morning, I didn't.

It was real foggy and I walked out to the well on tiptoe because I was barefoot and the ground was cold. So I was looking down at my feet all the time. And I got to the well, and I was looking down as I lowered the bucket. And when the bucket came up, I looked up.

Across the well from me, in the fog about five or six feet away, was this hairy thing. It was taller than me—well, almost everyone is taller than me—and it had big brown eyes. And it wasn't a man; it had long brown hair all over its body. And it just looked at me, almost sadly, like a dog might look at you. And I just stood there too scared to move.

It turned and went away into the fog. I stared after it for a long time and went in and locked the door. But it didn't really scare me, because it had those sad eyes.

105 *Lord of the LLano*

Out of the night, over the plains, snorting fire and brimstone comes the White Steed. His eyes glow like coals, the coals of a cowboy's campfire just before dawn. His hooves are steel, striking sparks off the stones. He throws back his head and calls his *manada* [harem] of mares. He is the lord of the *LLano* [the plain]. He is the *mestengo blanco*. He is the White Steed.

No cowboy can corral him. No lariat can lasso him. No rustler can ride him. He is the White Steed.

106a *Sally Baker*

I grew up in a small town in southwestern Arkansas, and about twenty miles south of my home, in Louisiana, is the little town of Cotton Valley. When I was growing up, I would often hear stories about a woman who had once lived in Cotton Valley, named Sally Baker; the story went around that she had been a witch. All the people who lived around her held her in awe and terror.

Children gathering blackberries along the road where she lived would disappear mysteriously. Weird sights could be seen around her tumbledown house when the moon was full. She had married seven times, each time by casting a spell on the man, and murdered them all by poison, burying each one in the woods around her house.

When she died, her evil was too strong to be bound by the walls of the grave. She was buried near the narrow dirt road that ran past her old home place, and the story went that if anyone was brave—or foolish—enough to go out there at night, and furthermore was so stouthearted—or stupid—as to run up and push over her gravestone, a spirit—the ghost of one of her husbands, still under her thrall—would emerge from the thick woods, white and glowing, to drive away the intruder and set the stone back up again. I spoke with at least one person who swore he had seen just that happen.

106b Sally Baker Debunked

The legend of Sally Baker is well known throughout the area I grew up in, and as I became old enough to drive and curious enough to wish to see such things for myself, I began to ask exactly where Sally Baker's grave was.

One day I happened to mention it in front of my father, and he said, sort of grumpily, "There's nothing to that story. Sally Baker was just an old widow woman."

I asked him how he knew that, and to my astonishment, he said that he had met Sally Baker himself. He and my mother had actually visited her in her house! I was taken aback: it was as if a maiden aunt had offhandedly mentioned that she used to date the Fouke Monster! I asked my father why he had never said anything about this before, and he replied, maddeningly, that he hadn't thought it was particularly important.

It seems that one day in the late 1940s, my mother and father and my two older brothers, who were just toddlers then, were out for an afternoon drive. My mother wasn't sure, but thought that they might have gone down Sally Baker's road looking for an oil rig that a friend of my father was working on. In any case, they came upon Sally Baker's house.

It was a small farm house with a little fenced dooryard and a shed off to one side. The grounds around were weedy and grown up, and the place had an unkept look about it. Even then, there were stories about Sally Baker and her weird ways. It was said that she was crazy and dangerous. But my father was very matter-of-fact and not one to believe all the gossip he heard, so, apparently on a whim, they decided to pay a call on Sally Baker, right then and there.

Looking back, my mother thought maybe it was the fact they had two little boys with them that got Sally Baker to come out. She normally did not talk to anybody except a niece who would bring groceries to her and look in on her. But come out she did. Everyone introduced themselves, Sally took on about the children, and they had a nice little talk.

Sally Baker was neither witch nor maniac, but merely an eccentric little old woman who was deathly afraid of people. She had indeed threatened children picking blackberries, but the threats were inspired by a fear that the children were going to do something to her. She invited my parents in, and they noticed that there was a hole cut into the ceiling in the front room. She explained that she was so frightened there all by herself that at night she would climb up into the loft and pull the ladder up after her.

Before my family left, she showed them around the place, letting my brothers play with the goats. She showed my father a 1936 Ford in the shed which had not been driven since her one husband had died years earlier—of natural causes. Finally, they all said goodbye and went on their way.

Not too many years after that, Sally Baker died and was buried there by her house. In the years that followed, the stories of her infamy grew and grew. I remember that when my parents told me all of this, I was disappointed. The truth, I felt then, made a much less interesting story than the legend about a witch.

Years later, when I was visiting home, I decided that I would finally go and find Sally Baker's grave. After asking around Cotton Valley, I got directions to it. The man who gave them to me chuckled about the whole thing. It seems that when his kids were teenagers, one of the big fun things to do was to drive ten or fifteen miles north to Springhill and find some poor sucker who didn't know any better and tell him the eerie story about Sally Baker's grave.

They would then drive the unsuspecting victim out to the gravesite, having first planted one of their friends out there with a sheet and a flashlight. After goading the out-of-towner to push over the gravestone, the "ghost" would emerge from the trees, moaning horribly, and the victim would usually react by screaming off down the road, telling all his friends the tale of horror and creating more suckers for subsequent evenings of entertainment.

I realized that if I had kept asking around when I was younger, chances are I would have ended up out there as the main feature one dark night.

My wife and I found the grave with no trouble, though it was far out in the lonely woods. It was near the road. There was no sign of where the house had been. There was a concrete slab covering the grave, but I don't know what the locals have the Springhill folks do now, as there was no gravestone there to knock over; it had apparently been stolen. All around the grave, the ground was packed down from foot traffic, and littered with broken beer bottles and other trash. There were the remains of a bonfire, apparently from a scare-party held on Hallowe'en night, which had been three or four days earlier.

After all these years, I had finally found Sally Baker's grave, and all I could think about was the real woman buried there amid the trash and beer bottles—that poor little old woman, so afraid of everyone that she hid in her loft at night.

And I wished that I had brought some flowers.

107 *Medicine-Meal Mush Boy*

There was once a great ghost spirit who came down into the *pueblo* and stole children. The People were afraid that some-day all the children would be gone. The elders met in the *kiva* and decided that the only way to rid themselves of this gigantic spirit would be to use spirit magic against it. The medicine men looked for some magic and a prayer to get rid of the ghost giant.

One of the medicine men went to the north, and he left a pouch of sacred corn meal that had been blessed. Another went to the east and left a pouch. Another went to the west and another to the south. When they returned and met, they did a song asking that all the pouches would be like a gate, closed, and that the giant ghost would not be able to get in to the *pueblo*. The magic did not work at this time [certain small changes were made at this point, by a pause] because people going out to pick piñon nuts saw a great pot on a fire up on the mesa rim. The people crept up along the mesa and hid behind pine trees and saw the ghost giant boiling water getting ready to eat another child.

The people ran back to the village, but the medicine men were all in the *kiva* at that time and there was no one to tell what they had seen, the medicine men not permitting anyone to disturb them in the *kiva*. The people ran about gathering cornmeal to put around their doorways in hopes that it would help keep the ghost giant away.

At sundown, the medicine men came out of the *kiva* and saw all the white cornmeal sprinkled around the houses; the people told about having seen the fire and the great pot, a basket coated with pitch.

One of the medicine men decided to take a pot of water into the *kiva* and put it on the shelf by the *sipapu* [the doorway from the Spirit World] and let it heat. He put white cornmeal in the pot and stirred it and made a poultice, and shaped it into the shape of a tiny boy. When he removed the cornmeal boy, by the *sipapu,* and blew it to cool it, the cornmeal-mush boy became alive and ran around him on the floor of the *kiva.* He picked up the cornmeal-mush boy and they went out of the *kiva* and out of the village.

The medicine man said to Mush Boy, "Go. Go and find the ghost giant."

Mush Boy ran up the side of the mesa to the place of the giant, but he was so small it took four days for him to go there. For four days, Father Sun shone on Mush Boy as he climbed, and the giant saw Mush Boy and caught him and put him in storage in a basket in his giant house and went to sleep. Mush Boy didn't seem like much of a threat.

But Mush Boy climbed out of the basket and went to the giant's arrow pouch. He took four arrows and the bow, and with all his magic strength, he shot the ghost giant four times. He went outside and kicked over the pot, and boiling water spilled over and ran in on the giant. Then Mush Boy ran in and melted in the boiling water, sending white corn meal through the four arrow holes into the ghost giant's heart, and killing him.

Medicine-meal Mush Boy had saved the People, and now they do a masked dance in his honor in the spring.

108 *The Ya-hah-nas at Mat-Sak-Ya*

At Mat-Sak-Ya Village, there were two ghost-spirits who saw, every night, children playing and wrestling near the *kivas* [meeting places of worship]. Children should be quiet and show respect near the *kivas.*

Because life was so good and the crops were so plentiful, the parents were always busy with the crops and seeing who could harvest the most, and they ignored the teaching of the children, and the children were becoming impolite and disrespectful.

These ya-hah-nas, these spirits, were watching the children with great sadness and disapproval. They knew that when disrespect comes, other bad things come. So the ya-hah-nas went down and went to Koh-thlou-wah-la-wah and told them that the children of Mat-sak-ya were being disrespectful to the ancestors. The ya-hah-nas wanted to punish the children and show them the error of their ways. They had a dreamsleep, and they decided that the next evening they would wash up, and after they had combed their hair, they would put on human clothes and would paint their faces the way the People do to portray *katsinas* [or *kachinas*].

The ya-hah-nas looked very handsome dressed and painted like the People. The two were ready to leave and come up from the Spirit World into the *kiva*, when the leaders of the ya-hah-nas came up with some instructions, and the sacred smoke was made (which you have to make to come up from the Spirit World—you come up in the smoke). They were to leave a home-rolled cigarette and make marks on the floor with corn meal, and in that number of days [as shown by the number of corn-meal stripes], some punishment would come to any children who had been disrespectful.

The ya-hah-nas came into the *kiva* [here some details were omitted with a pause], and they climbed the ladder out into the village. When some of the rude children came by loudly arguing and wrestling when they should have been at home in bed, one of the ya-hah-nas who had a liking for children came out and called to them in a scolding but loving way, "Stop this. Show the proper respect for your ancestors." But the children thought it was just one of the men of the village and they threw dirt at the spirit, and he went back into the *kiva* sadly.

Then the children looked down into the *kiva* and saw sacred corn meal at the foot of the ladder and saw the *katsinas* in the good light inside, and they knew that these were ya-hah-nas. They ran away, and one older boy went to his father and told him what he had seen. The father frowned thoughtfully and followed the boy back to the *kiva*.

The father went down into the *kiva*. He found the home-rolled cigarette and he blessed it. By blessing it, he also blessed the ya-hah-nas, to counter any magic that the spirit had planned against the children.

After the number of days given, the ancestor-spirits were going to put their costumes on and have a dance in the *kiva*. One of the ancestors did not paint himself but rather put on a mask of black powder. They started singing the song in the *kiva*. As they sang, the elder lead-singer changed the song to a song about women, for the mother and mother's family were the ones responsible for teaching the children the traditional ways. The song sang about catching a woman. On the way out of the *kiva*, the ancestor with the black mask caught a young woman. When he touched her and let go of her, she became empowered by him.

The woman knew what was wrong in the village and how the People had failed to teach the children and how punishment would come on the children. She knelt and begged the ancestor in the black mask to put the punishment on her and not on the children. She was allowed to go into the *kiva* with the ancestors, and she went with them into the Spirit World, leaving her dead body behind in the *kiva*. The brave young woman gave herself for the People's good.

When the men of the village went down into the *kiva*, the body was there, and they knew all that had happened. The people mended their ways and taught the children respect. But if they ever forget again, the ya-hah-nas will come.

109 Ghost Train

The little mining town of Mayer, Arizona, didn't think much about a mining train thundering through town in 1893 on its way to one of the nearby smelters, but folks noticed something about this train: it passed through without an engine. The story telegraphed to mining towns as far away as Crown King and Cleator that a runaway train had rolled through Mayer. The story grew when, a few hours later, the train came back through from the opposite direction...Mayer sat in a basin, and the train looked as if it would just roll back and forth through town "forever"!

On its third pass through town a couple of retired railroad men jumped on the train and set the brakes. The mystery train skidded to a stop at the edge of town. All the mines and railyards were telegraphed: no one claimed the runaway train. It sat there for days; then, one morning, it was gone.

No one heard an engine, no one saw the train leave. It vanished in the night without a sound and without a trace. The story circulated around Yavapai County, until one old miner offered an explanation. Old copies of the Mayer *Daily Progress* confirmed the miner's story: in 1871 twenty-two miners had escaped the Iron King mine flood disaster by crowding onto the engine of mine train No. 22; they uncoupled the engine and steamed out just as the remaining cars sank below the black water. Twenty years before, twenty-two men rode to safety on an engine without a train—twenty-two years later old No. 22 came back to earth—a train without an engine!

110 *Bloodsucker*

Down by the Rio Grande, we have mosquitos in great quantity. It all began at twilight when this horrible ghost would go up and down the Rio Grande many years ago. This ghost would come upon people who were walking up or down the river, and suck all the blood out of their bodies. It was terrible, and no one could stop it.

There was then a young Indian man who had married a beautiful woman. In the cool of the afternoon she gave birth to a beautiful baby girl. Now, the father had come from the old pueblo of Oke-Oyunke, but that place had flooded several times; the young man had built his house by the river on the east side, near the pueblo of Yunque-Yunque. The house was high above the riverbed but all alone. In this house, the girl was born, and the young man wanted to take his daughter down and show her to his family.

He started to go, but his wife said, "No. You can't go down there in the evening because of the spirit that goes up and down the river!" On the next day, the man went to get wood and did things to care for his wife. This was the time when the sisters should come. He wanted to go down to the pueblo and tell her sisters about the baby, because they were the ones who would name the baby.

But his wife didn't want him to leave her, because if he left early in the morning, he wouldn't be coming back for a long time. They waited until four days had passed, until she was healthier and the baby was strong and it was the time for the mother to go through the first cleansing ceremony. The three went down to the pueblo to do the ceremony there; they went down that day and had the ceremony.

But the young man's mother was very superstitious, and she said that until the child had been given its own name, it should sleep in the house in which it had been born. So the three left, and were walking along the river just as the sun was going down. The man and wife were quarreling about the traditions and why he had built the house so far out, and they were just about to cross the little footbridge, not seeing that it was getting to be twilight.

The man was on the bridge, and the spirit came down the riverbank like the wind and took the blood from the woman and the baby. There was nothing he could do, and the young man ran to his house filled with anger and grief. He sat there all night and asked the spirits to give him strength.

He took the sacred corn meal and rubbed it on his face, and finally he knew what to do. He spent all the next day making spears. Many very sharp spears. Then he followed the trail of blood droplets on the grass along the river until he came to a cave. This was where the spirit stayed in daylight.

He took the spears and drove their shafts in the dirt with their points inward, ringing the cave mouth. Then, at twilight, he stood across the river and called out with a wailing sound and called out the spirit-that-sucks-blood. The spirit came out like the wind.

As the spirit hit the spear points, it was cut into thousands of pieces—and each of those pieces became a mosquito. So now, when you go down to the Rio Grande, between Oke-Oyunke and Yunque-Yunque, where the Indian paintbrush grows, there are mosquitos there, and they will suck the blood right out of you!

111 *Joe and the Devil*

Years ago, one of our hands, named Joe, had a drinking problem. His wife always begged him not to drink hard liquor so much; she took him to church a lot, and the priest warned him that if he didn't stop drinking hard liquor, someday the Devil would come for his soul.

He had been drinking a little beer, and sometimes he would drink a little wine, but one day he got a-hold of some hard liquor and had been drinking it, and he was driving home. He rolled down the window and threw the liquor bottle out, but the wind blew the empty bottle back in and it hit him in the head. Just then he saw a black top hat in his rear-view mirror.

He was still facing front, but he was craning his neck all around looking in the rear-view mirror from every angle to see what he could see; but he couldn't see anything. He finally turned around for a quick look over his shoulder. There in the back seat was a man wearing a top hat and a tuxedo. He was driving pretty fast down the road, and he had to look back ahead, but he was craning all around trying to see who was in his back seat, in the rear-view mirror. But he couldn't see him in the mirror.

He slowed down to a crawl, and turned around in his seat. There behind him sat a man in a tuxedo, pulling long, black gloves out of the pocket of his coat, as though he was getting ready to put on his gloves and get out of the car when it stopped. The man was just about to put on the glove, and Joe saw that instead of a human hand, the man had a cloven hoof that came into view slowly as he was about to draw the second glove on.

Joe slowed the car even more, now almost to a stop, and turned back around with horror and fascination to see what the man was doing. Now he saw a woman all dressed in white seated beside the man in black; she was staring at Joe sternly and disapprovingly. The man in black now had both gloves on, and looked normal, but he, too, was staring sternly at Joe with eyes that glowed red like a fire. Joe pulled over to the side of the road, stopped the car, slid across the front seat, and threw open the passenger door.

Joe knelt at the running board with his knees in the sand and his elbows on the car and began to pray in a loud voice as fast as he could. He recited the "Hail, Mary" over and over and over. After several minutes of prayer, the rear passenger door opened, and the man stepped out into the sand. Joe saw his feet under the door. Instead of fancy dress shoes, the man had large cloven hooves. The hooves left deep imprints in the sand as he—the thing—walked away from the car and into the *bosque* [woods].

Joe stayed there and prayed for a long time after that, with his eyes closed. When he was sure he was alone and safe, he got up and drove home. He told the story to men who didn't believe him, and he offered to take them to the place and he would show them the hoofprints, which he said were still in the sand by the arroyo.

Joe never took another drink of hard liquor again.

112   *The Wild White Mare*

There's a weird ghost story told at Española, about the rodeo: it tells of Don Paulo, who would arrive the day before the rodeo in Española in July. He would have one white stallion and one white mare in his trailer. He brought them for the [wild horse] roping contest, and no one was ever able to rope them.

One roper came up from Texas, the best lasso man around, to compete in the contest, and I know the story to be true because my uncle was there! Everyone lined up [in the Spanish-style arena] to rope Don Paulo's white stallion and Don Paulo's wild white mare. The Texan joined the line-up. None of the first ropers could even come close—it was as if the rope moved away at the last moment. Then it was the Texan's turn.

The Texan rode a shiny, polished bay; his saddle was elegantly tooled, and he had a rope the likes of which no one had ever seen before. It didn't look coiled; it was a square-braided rope. He went after the mare first. He threw his lasso high into the air and it landed right around the mare's neck. As he jerked on the lasso to tighten it, the rope cut right through the mare's neck and the mare's head came right off!

But that didn't stop the ghostly mare. She jumped over the fence and galloped into the trees which are by Ranchitos, between Española and the rodeo grounds at San Juan Pueblo. And my uncle said that you can hear this ghostly wild white mare whinny at night. Right after this happened, she didn't make a sound, but through the years her whinny is getting stronger and stronger...because her head is growing back!

113 Stampede Mesa

In the stormy autumn of 1889 a trail herd of over a thousand steers moved up the Blanco River [in Crosby County, Texas] and the drovers chose to let the herd overnight on level ground at the top of a mesa after watering at the Blanco. The outfit was bedded down under a threatening sky when the night guards came upon a lone cowpoke cutting out some cattle in the dark. The man claimed he was cutting out some unbranded mavericks of his own that had drifted into the outfit's passing herd.

The night guards didn't believe him, and didn't bother to check. The lone cowboy was tied up in the saddle and his horse led under a low tree on the mesa rim. A lynching rope was over the branch and the night guards ready to hang the rider when a flash of lightning and loud roll of thunder spooked the horse. In a bolt the horse and its hapless rider went over the edge and disappeared into the dark canyon below. The night guards were shaken; it wasn't supposed to have happened like this.

Deep in the darkest night, the thunder and lightning came again, and spooked the herd. The outriders tried to mill the herd to a halt, the death of the supposed rustler still on their minds. Then, in a bright flash of lightning they saw him: the ghost of the dead cowboy, white as lightning, riding bigger than life through the herd. The herd spooked again, and in a thundering stampede, a thousand cattle and the lynch-happy outriders went over the cliff in the raging storm.

No herd ever held on that mesa again survived. They were always stampeded by some unseen force. Sometimes trail riders saw the ghost of the lone, misjudged cowboy in lightning that startled their herd. Sometimes, in late evening, when the sun cut across the mesa onto low storm clouds, trail riders saw the ghost and the ghostly herd standing high as a mountain moving across the storm clouds. And sometimes they saw the murderous night guards, huge and hellish, riding with the stampeding herd across the storm clouds, damned to ride drag forever across Stampede Mesa.

114   Corpse Walkers

When a person dies, his body is an empty shell. If the body is left unburied, it is like an empty house that an evil spirit can enter and live among the Living People. This is why one must bury a body, and the [Buddhist] monks will bury any body that they find very quickly. But the monks do another thing with a dead body, also.

In the mountainous regions, if someone dies high on a narrow trail where the way is too steep and narrow for two men to carry the body out, and the family does not want the body buried in the high mountains, then they call the monks who are Corpse Walkers. The Corpse Walkers go up the trail to the body, and they put their spirit into it, and they come back down the trail with the corpse walking, more like hopping, stiffly along behind them. This is in Old China, but it is spoken of in America among the Chinese of California.

115   The Spirit in the Milk Shed

An Hispano man told this story to my friend, who told it to me:

When I was a boy, I wanted to go to the dance. My father said that I should not go, then he ordered me not to go, but I went anyway. When I came back from the dance, my father was waiting for me on the porch of the house, with his rifle across his lap. It was late, but I had not done my chores before the dance, so he said to me, "Go milk the cow."

I said, "Well, can't I have a lantern to go out to milk the cow?" and he said, "You disobeyed me. You don't deserve a lantern. Just milk the cow in the dark." So I went out and got the cow and led her to the shed where the milking was done. When I got partway into the dark, dark shed, the cow planted her hooves, stood firm and lowered her head, and refused to go into the shed. She began to blow [to snort] as though she was angry or afraid.

I began to be afraid; I went into the shed, and saw a light above me in this small shed. I looked up, and there was a beautiful woman dressed in white hovering in the air above me.

She said, *"No tengas miedo; soy tu madre. No permito que nada te haga daño.* [Do not be afraid; I am your mother. I will not permit anything to harm you.]" When she said that, the cow relaxed, walked on into the shed, put its head into the yoke and began to eat the feed that was there. I took the pan and milked the cow. I remember distinctly the sound that each squirt of milk made against the metal of the pan.

I went back to the house, and there was my father, still angry with me for going to the dance against his orders. I brought the milk into the house, and explained to my father that the cow had not wanted to go into the shed, frightened by something. But then I had seen the spirit of my mother. She had told me not to be afraid, that she was my mother, and that she would not allow anything to happen to me.

My father embraced me, and held me very close, and wept.

He said we should return to the shed together, to see if she was still there, so that he could tell her how much he loved her, for she had died about two years before and he missed her terribly, as did I. We went out to the shed, and when we walked into the shed this time, instead of the spirit, there was hovering in midair a black catafalque, resembling the carriage body of a horse-drawn hearse, with the decorations and the black curtains but with no wheels and no team of horses.

One of the black curtains was pulled back, and my father looked in. Lying inside was the body of my mother. He told her that he missed her and that he would always love her. Then he and I walked out, and just as we were in the doorway, we looked back for one last glimpse at the catafalque, but the shed was empty.

116 *The Holy Spirit and the Blind Man*

There was once a three-tiered spire on the Church of San Miguel [in Santa Fe], but a great and mysterious storm blew it down, with its great bell along with it. The spire, which had been a fairly recent addition, was not built back. The bell was left much where it had fallen and now hangs by a buffalo hide *reata* [braided rope] woven by one of the custodians of the Church about a hundred years ago. It is the oldest bell in America, cast in Andalusia [in Spain] in the year of Our Lord 1356. It bears the legend "Saint Joseph Pray For Us." It bears another legend that is told aloud.

A century ago [the bell fell in 1872], a blind man came to pray every day at noontime. While he was praying, sometimes, even though no one was present at the bellrope yet to ring it, the old bell would begin to toll. As it rang, impelled by the Spirit, the blind man could see and describe and point to the icons in the chapel. When the tolling ceased, he was blind again. Ringing the bell by its rope had no effect on his sight. Only the miraculous ringing restored his sight. And that is the story of the Holy Ghost and the blind man.

117 *Wham-Slam-Jenny-Mo-Jam*

Once upon a time, there were a little boy and a little girl whose maternal grandmother was said to be a witch. People said the old witch had a magic ball that she used to hunt down children. The boy and his sister were so curious to know if what they had heard was true that they begged their mother to let them go visit the old woman. When their mother heard that the children wanted to go and spend the night with the old woman who had raised her, she became worried.

"No, my dear children," she warned, "you cannot go, for no child has ever returned from that place but me."

When the boy and his sister began to cry, the mother finally consented to let them go if they would be very careful and remember the few good magic spells she had already taught them.

They kissed their mother good-bye, and before they left the boy said, "I will put my twelve dogs in their pen, but if we are in danger, I will whistle the magic call that only they can hear. If my dogs begin to bark for no apparent reason, let them out and they will come to our rescue."

It was about noon when the children started out for their grandmother's house in the thicket, and before long, they found her working in her twisted garden. When she saw the children, she clapped her hands with glee. She asked them their names.

"I'm Jenny," said the girl.

"I'm Mo," said the boy.

She invited them to come into her yard and play with her own children, who were about the same size and age as Jenny and Mo, but whose ears were just a little too pointed and furry, and whose teeth were just a little too long and sharp.

The children played in the yard, but the old woman's children didn't know any of the right games. Meanwhile, the old woman was sharpening on her grindstone a sharp knife she had taken from her belt. Mo helped her by turning the grindstone while she sharpened the knife.

"What are you going to do with this knife?" asked Mo.

She answered, "I'm going to kill a wild hog."

She built a large fire beneath an old iron kettle and filled it with water. Soon the water was boiling and boiling. By this time the sun had set, and the old woman told all four children to eat the cornpone on the table in the house and go on upstairs and get ready for bed. She followed them and showed them which pallet to sleep on. To her own children, she gave a dark bedsheet, and to Jenny and Mo she gave a white sheet. Pretty soon her children were asleep and snoring in a grunting sort of way, and Jenny dozed off, too, but Mo was afraid to go to sleep.

The old witch told him to go to sleep, but he replied, "When I'm at home and can't sleep, my mother gives me my fiddle to play."

The old woman brought him a fiddle from off the mantlepiece. Then she sat down at the bottom of the stairs and waited with her long knife hidden beneath her apron. As Mo played the sweetest songs he knew, the old woman fell asleep. He could hear her snoring. Quietly he awoke Jenny. Together they spread the white sheet over the other children, and put things from around the room under the dark sheet to make it look like someone was asleep under it, too.

Tiptoeing past the sleeping witch, the children headed for home in the moonlight. Pretty soon the witch woke up and went to the white sheet and killed the wild children. When she lighted a candle and found she'd killed her own children, she was very angry.

Immediately she went to the cupboard and took down her glass ball. She flew to the door and down to the path. She rolled the ball down one path, but soon it came back, and she knew the children had not gone that way. Next she rolled it down the other way. When the ball did not come back, she knew that was the way the children had gone.

The children heard the magic ball rumbling along the ground and figured the witch was coming, so they climbed a catalpa tree. At the top of the tree, Mo gave the whistle for his dogs. Back at his house the dogs began to bark, and the mother came and turned them out.

Soon the witch came with an axe and began chopping down the tree.

As she chopped, she chanted, "Wham-Slam-Jenny-Mo-Jam! Wham-Slam-Jenny-Mo-Jam!"

The chips flew in all directions as the axe fell again and again. As the chips flew, Mo chanted, "Catalpa Tree, when the axe goes 'Chop!' grow big at the bottom, grow little at the top! Catalpa Tree, when the axe goes 'Chop!' grow big at the bottom, grow little at the top!"

Every time a chip fell out, another one grew back. But the witch kept chopping and chanting. It wasn't long before the twelve dogs came running toward the witch. They yelped and jumped and tried to bite her, but her long knife killed all except one last dog. He jumped at her throat and sank his teeth in and killed her. After the old witch was dead, the children came down and cut the witch's heart out and rubbed it on the noses of the dead dogs, and they all came back to life.

The children and the dogs walked home and got there just as the sun came up.

118 *Booger Deer*

Near Cantil, California, in the Kelso Valley, hunters have shot at a huge deer that bullets do not touch. He's a magnificent stag, of the like not seen in this country since the Indian days of the 1500s, and you can't kill him no matter how hard you try. You see, he's already dead.

The Booger Deer of Shepp Springs was first seen in the 1930s, larger than life. Every deer hunter covets that rack for a trophy, but bullets can't touch him. He leaves no trail of blood even when the finest marksman shoots at him. He doesn't even leave spoor.

How could he? He's a ghost.

119 *Creature-in-the-Hole*

Before the Europeans came to this country, the Indians saw a great water panther in the Red River above Heber Springs. This ancient spirit-monster lives forever and has killed any number of people as sustenance. Frontiersmen, then loggers, then later hunters, were killed and eaten by the thing. Down through the years the legend persisted.

When Greer's Ferry was impounded by a dam, the last time I heard the story [about 1961], was when some friends of mine and I were in a car trying to scientifically "observe" the "dragon of the Little Red River." A drowning victim's body had not ever been found in spite of searches that year, and the monster was blamed for "pulling" the victim under and consuming the evidence. The older boys said the creature had been spotted—always using the latest technological update in legends—at or near its den, a hole or cave on an island in the river, before the dam created the lake. The supposition was that now, with the creature's lair two hundred feet below the surface of the lake, the creature would no longer be a threat.

But no! A scuba diver reported having his mask ripped off by a creature coming out of a hole—the "Creature in the Hole." Senator John McClelland had a house built on the shores, incorporating a natural cave as his boat house, with an elevator being installed in a sinkhole that connected the cave with the hillside above. The workers installing the elevator were said to have heard the creature's unearthly cries late at night, echoing up the sinkhole as if the thing were just below them in the cave.

And hungry.

If you're ever out on Greer's Ferry Lake at night at this time of year [around Hallowe'en] fishing in your boat, and you hear the distant cries of the water birds, and you see the forms moving in the shimmering water, remember this story.

120 *Changing Man*

My mother used to run a boarding house in Arkansas. One of our boarders was a man named Wesley Paddy. I called him Pa Paddy. He swore this story happened to him in central Arkansas around the turn of the century. There was a bandit who robbed travelers. He was tracked back to a house deep in the woods, and the sheriff and a posse surrounded the house and called for him to come out. Shots were exchanged, and in a practice common in those times, a lantern was lit and thrown in through a window.

The house caught fire as intended, and a huge black dog came running out the front door. The posse ignored it and waited for the house to burn to the ground. In the ashes, there was absolutely no sign of a corpse. Pa Paddy was in the posse and explained very calmly that the robber must have been a changing man, who could change into animal form. He told me that as the plain and simple truth.

121 *Three Nephites*

Jesus Christ came to South America during his ministry here on earth and gathered followers just as He had in the Holy Land; three of these Nephites asked Him for the same blessing John the Beloved had, that is, that they would not pass away until He had come into his Kingdom. The Nephites broke away from their sinful brothers, the lazy and quarrelsome Lamanites, and the Three Nephites are still seen in North America around Utah.

One lady picked up a hitchhiker near here [Ogden, Utah], and while he was riding—in the back seat—he warned her to set aside enough food and supplies to last for two years, because there was to be—is to be—a time of trouble, and she should be prepared. When she tried to ask him questions, he didn't answer. When she looked in the rear-view mirror, she couldn't see him. When she turned around, he was gone!

122 Killer-of-the-Alien-Gods

The Dineh hero Killer-of-the-Alien-Gods [who along with his brother had killed Yeitso and other Evil Giants and cut off their heads and left them as landmarks at Tshotshihl, to become *el Cabezón* and the smaller hummocks near Mount San Mateo] went out to find another evil demon he had heard of. A ghoul named He-Who-Kicks-People-Down-Cliffs lived on a trail on Gray Mesa, and Killer-of-the-Alien-Gods heard of him and set out to find him and kill him.

The Hero walked along a trail, and where the trail grew narrow, he saw an ugly old man reclining on a rock just above the trail, seeming to be asleep. The old man seemed harmless, and as the Hero started to walk past below him on the narrow part of the trail, the old man suddenly kicked one leg out at him. The Hero stepped back, dodging the kick.

"Old One," said the Hero, "why did you kick at me?"

"My son," said the ugly man, "I did not kick at you. I only stretched my leg out as I turned to sun myself."

The Hero Killer-of-the-Alien-Gods started again to pass the old man on the narrow part of the trail. Again the old man kicked at him, but he dodged the kick and stepped back. A third and fourth time the Hero tried to pass and the old one kicked at him. The Hero knew that this was the demon he had sought.

The Hero took out his stone knife and killed the demon with a blow to the forehead, but the body did not fall from its resting place on the rock even though the demon was dead and the rock face was steep. The Hero looked under the body; the demon's long hair grew into the rock face like roots.

The Hero cut the demon's hair and the corpse slid off the rock face, off the trail, and down the cliff face out of sight below. At once the Hero heard snarling and growling and quarreling below. When he went ahead on the trail, he found that it led to nowhere.

Killer-of-the-Alien-Gods went back the way he came, past the rock face with the hair-roots, hearing the sounds of animals feeding below him, to another trail that led down the cliff face to the valley floor. There he saw twelve ugly children of the demon, devouring their father's corpse. "This would have been my body they ate of," thought the Killer-of-the-Alien-Gods, "if he had kicked me down the cliff."

The Hero took his knife and killed eleven of the ugly children, whose mouths were dripping with the gore and blood of their father, but one child ran swiftly away up into the rocks. Killer-of-the-Alien-Gods chased the ghoul-child to the top of the rocks, but when he looked upon the ghoul-child, he said, "You ran from me so swiftly that I chased you, thinking you might be a creature worthy of killing. Now I see that you are just an ugly eater of dead flesh like your brothers. I will let you live." And he went away.

The People were never again troubled by alien gods, and the one ghoul-child lived on the rocks and became the father of the carrion birds that live on the mesa rim today.

123 White Riders

Along the Gila River in Arizona, they tell the story of two ranchhands traveling along the Diablo Trail who got caught in a two-day sandstorm. They holed up in an outcropping of rock beside a dry water hole. By the second day, their horses had dropped over dead and were covered with sand, their food was gone, and they'd been out of water for a solid day.

Gradually, the storm grew quiet, though the two cowpokes couldn't see any letup in the wind and sand. Then, out of the distant wall of sand came a lone rider, dressed in white, on a white horse. Behind him came a long line of riders, single file, twelve of them, dressed in pure white.

Their spurs and belt buckles were silver, the bits and snaffles and curb chains were silver. Their boots were white cowhide; their shirts and trousers were white linen; their hats were white fur felt. They rode in slow, leading a thirteenth white horse.

Two of the white riders got down and lifted one of the stranded ranchhands up from the sand and helped him onto the riderless horse. The other fellow called to them through his dry throat and begged them to take him, too.

As the line of riders disappeared back into the storm, the last rider turned and smiled at the cowpoke left behind. "Sorry," he said, "it's just not your time yet."

The other hand passed out from thirst; when he woke up, he was back at the ranch. His bunkmates had found him still alive after the storm died, but his partner was dead in the sand.

124 Hopi Bones

I once worked for the Museum of Northern Arizona, founded by Dr. Colton and his wife. One of Dr. Colton's informants was a Hopi who was a member of the Masau Clan. Bloody-faced Masau is the god who has given the Hopi permission to live in this world; his visage is a partially-decomposed face, and members of his clan have as their special privilege the ability to talk with the dead.

There is an area of the old part of the museum where the physical anthropology collection is housed. [The Hopi informant] told me not to go there at night. The spirits of the dead who were evil return to those bones at night—especially, I believe, in October. At night, he says, you can feel the presence of many spirits and hear them converse. It is best not to go in there at all, but if you do go in, you should offer apologies and an offering of cornmeal or pollen.

125 Monster of the Mogollón Rim

Before the turn of the century, some miners went out on the Mogollón Rim searching for gold. Knowing that miners going into the Superstition Mountains to the south often did not return, these men were watchful of any Indians, fearing an attack. The miners came upon women and children at a waterhole and killed them all to keep them from reporting the miners' whereabouts and number. One miner was a lazy thief who bummed off his friends, and he stole from the dead bodies.

The brothers and fathers of the dead women and children scouted along the Mogollón Rim until they caught up to the miners. They killed the miners, and the miner who was carrying things stolen from the women he had killed was hung up by his hands and skinned. The Indian men left him for dead, but he did not die. As he hung there from a ledge, he stretched and stretched until the rope broke and he fell to the ground.

Now he walks the Rim at night. He is eight feel tall and has no skin. He's still looking for gold, and he "gets" any Boy Scouts that wander away from their camp and kills them for the gold and silver fillings in their teeth.

Possessed By Spirits
(Including Stories of People Driven by the Sight of Ghosts)

126 Mary Calhoun

Once there came from Ireland a family by the name of Calhoun. The eldest child was the daughter Mary, the apple of her father's eye. And one day, passing through the graveyard on the top of hills near their house, the father of the family stopped to rest on a sarcophagus and watch the sun go down. When he got up and walked on, the old man was so refreshed that he forgot his walking stick.

At the house, where the supper table was all but laid, he mentioned his walking stick, and Mary said she'd go back and get it and be to the house again in a shake. Out the door she went, before anyone could stop her.

Entering the graveyard, she walked toward the sarcophagus her father had mentioned, and there she found the walking stick leaning up against a stone. She bent down to pick it up, and noticed in the moonlight an old, broken-down grave at her feet.

It was an old grave, and it been dug shallow, as if those who dug it were in haste or as if there was no family to re-mound the grave when the coffin inevitably collapsed and the grave caved in. As she stood there, staring fixedly at the cracks in the ground, a bony white hand reached up out of the grave and grasped the hem of her dress.

She started to let out a scream, but she found she could not. Out came another hand, and grabbed her dress higher up. And slowly, something very, very old and dead climbed up her garment until it sat on her shoulders.

"Walk," said the Thing in a voice like wind in dry autumn leaves.

And Mary Calhoun walked, against her will, held in thrall by the power of the Thing. Down the lane they went, towards the houses along the path beyond the fallow field. The Thing on her shoulders was light, like husks at shocking time, but it was also heavy, with the weight of unspeakable evil buried in the cold earth for a century or more.

"I'm hungry," said the Thing, "for I've not et in many a year."

"Turn in here," said the Thing at the first house. Then, "No, turn away! There's holy water in this house!"

At the next house, "Turn in here." Then, "No, turn away! There's holy water here, on garments blessed at Mass!"

At the third house, "Turn in here... Go in, for there's no holy water in this house."

Inside, Mary found that all the family, neighbors whom she knew well, were fast in bed. Somehow time had flown for them but crawled for her as she had stared at that broken-down grave.

"Go to kitchen." She went, all unwilling.

"Get a knife and a bowl." She got as she was bidden.

"Upstairs." She went up, with the Thing a-riding her shoulders. In the loft slept the three fine sons of the family, Mary's childhood playmates. "Cut their throats!" And with trembling hands and tears in her eyes, Mary cut the boys' throats.

When the first drop of blood fell into the bowl, each boy stirred. With the second drop, each boy grew cold and still. With the third drop, each boy was ashen and dead. Mary took the blood in the bowl and returned to the kitchen.

"Make gruel," said the Thing, and she did. When the water was boiled, and oatmeal and the blood poured in, the Thing commanded, "Serve us."

Mary took two bowls and spoons from the cupboard, and napkins from the dry sink, and the bowl of bloodied oatmeal from the stove, and set the table.

"Now, take a morsel," the Thing bade her. Mary's hand shook as she lifted a spoonful of the horrid gruel toward her mouth; her hand shook so violently that she dropped the bite into her kerchief at her neck, where it could not be seen. The spoon went on up to her lips. Her jaws worked and her throat swallowed, all against her will.

"Now that you've et in the house of the Dead, you're one of us." The Thing climbed slowly down and sat at table, unaware that Mary had not eaten the morsel. When it let go of her garment, its power over her faded away, but Mary was a clever lass, and sat down stiffly and pretended to eat as if the spell still held her.

As the Thing slavered and drooled and ate away at the bowl of gruel, Mary lifted spoonful after spoonful towards her mouth, and when the Thing was not looking, she dropped each bite into the folds of the kerchief at her breast. When both their bowls were empty, the Thing stood up and said, "We'll leave now."

"I'll take up first," said Mary, and she took the bowls, the serving bowl, the spoons and the napkins to the dry sink in the kitchen. She took off her kerchief, folded it over the gruel, and set it in the sink. When she returned to the parlor, the Thing climbed her dress again, and sat on her shoulders. The powerful spell returned and Mary did as it bade her.

"Back to the graveyard!" And they went out onto the path and past the houses towards the fallow land.

"Now you're one of us, you can know what the Dead know," the Thing said. "That gruel made you one of us, but if any had been left and fed to those dead boys, why, they'd rise up alive again."

A little further along the Thing said, all chatty-like, "That cairn of stones there: under it I hid all my gold—ill-gotten in life, but little good it did me."

Back in the graveyard, Mary saw the sun was about to rise. Time had flown again as they ate their gruesome meal. The Thing climbed down, and Mary felt the spell fading away.

"Come down, Mary Calhoun, into your new home."

"I'll not come down," Mary cried, "for I've et none of your hideous gruel!"

The Thing let out a terrible oath and started to climb back out of its grave and clutch at her dress. The sun rose over the hill and sunlight struck the Thing. Mary grabbed her father's walking stick and struck the Thing. It flew into a thousand sparkling shards like husk or vellum, and the sun rose over the graveyard. Mary took her father's walking stick and started home.

She turned in at the third house, where the family was awake and wailing their sons' fate. Mary went in and spoke with the father. "There's fever hereabouts, perhaps they've only swooned."

"Ah, you're daft, Mary Calhoun," said the father of the boys, "I know dead when I see it!" Still and all, he let Mary go to the kitchen, where she got a bowl of water and her kerchief, as if to mop the boys' fevered brows. Upstairs, she fed them the oatmeal. With the first morsel, each boy stirred. With the second bite, each boy blinked and awoke, and with the third bite each boy sat up and yawned or stretched and said, "What terrible nightmares I've had."

Mary Calhoun lived a long and comfortable life, and she came into some money later on, after she'd saved for years and bought the fallow land beside the graveyard. But throughout her life, no matter who died, rich or poor, great or small, her friend or not, she never went to the burial. In fact, she never, ever, went into that graveyard again.

127   *The Possessed Girl at McKinney*

When I was a boy, the youngest of three sons, we lived near Celina, Texas, not far from the larger and better-known town of McKinney. There, when I was a teenager, the McKinney newspapers said that a young woman had become possessed by an evil spirit. The whole county was soon talking about it. In the dark of night, dried beans flew around the room where the girl was. Things flew through the air and clattered off the walls. The girl lay in bed and moaned and thrashed at times. In daylight hours, or when the lamps were lit, the spirit manifested itself in other ways.

The gossip said that three old women called sisters, all dressed in black, had come from the local spiritualist group to "assist" the family in its time of need. The sisters began to hold séances, and in the daytime, or if the room was lit, the sisters would call upon the spirit to knock on the table, on a wall, or on some other piece of wood. We knew two young men who had been to see the possessed girl, as half the population of the county must have done, and they told us all about trying to debunk the spirit knocking.

These two boys claimed to have tried two different ways to get at the truth or falsehood of the event. On their visit, while a séance was being held in the sitting room of the house, one of the boys went down under the house, where the floor joists sat up two feet off the ground on rock pillars, and crawled around looking for signs of fraud. He found nothing but cobwebs. Later, up inside the house itself, during the same séance, one cousin tried to trick the "sisters." He asked them to call upon the "spirit" to knock inside a solid wood door, thinking that would be impossible to fake. He stood at the half-open door, and touched it lightly from both sides with the tips of all ten fingers. Sure enough, when the "sisters" called for it, he jumped away from the door and claimed to have felt the knocking—which everyone in the room had heard—inside the door!

My brothers and I and all the boys in our town sat endless hours in the shade of a tree or porch, telling and retelling all we had heard about the possessed girl and speculating about the "spirit" and what-all it could and could not do. Finally, we determined that we would all go to McKinney ourselves and prove or disprove this supernatural event once and for all.

Unfortunately, none of us had a car.

For almost a week we worked on Fred, an older boy with a Model-T Ford, trying to convince him to take us to McKinney to see this possessed girl. Unfortunately, Fred was somewhat easily alarmed, to put it mildly, and he wanted no part of the whole adventure. After long hours of cajoling and pleading, collecting nickels to buy his gasoline for the trip, and promising like a bunch of Tom Sawyers to do all manner of favors for him, Fred's sissiness was overcome by his basic greed. The trip was on!

The appointed time and day came, after dark. This was dictated by the fact that the possessed girl got "wound up" more after dark, and the dried bean crop took to the air with the lamps blown out, and by the even more crucial fact that

Fred worked by day. My brothers and I and more local teenaged boys than wisdom would allow piled into the Model T and began the trek across dirt roads to McKinney. Being the youngest of the crowd, I was squashed over against the side wall with no door, with about half my anatomy hanging outside the car. It was awkward, but the night breeze was pleasant.

With the darkness deepening around us, we began to talk about the possessed girl and the "sisters" and the knocking and the séances and the beans. We were equally divided into two camps: one camp averred that anyone could throw dried beans in the dark, and in fact, some of them had done it before; the other camp retaliated with the inexplicable knocking.

"I'll bet that old spirit could knock anywhere it wanted," said one of the town boys. "I'll bet he could even knock right here in this motorcar!"

Well, at that point the temptation was too great.

With the half of my anatomy that was hanging out of the car, I knocked on the side wall three…loud…knocks.

The reaction ranged from yelps to laughter, but the worst possible thing happened. Fred went white as a bedsheet, grabbed the brake and threw it on, skidded the car to a stop, and headed back toward Celina. No amount of explanation, pleading, or apologizing would make him go to McKinney, that or any other night.

Well, I was a worse outcast than a leper for days after that, and my brothers and I secretly plotted revenge on the sissy.

There was a blacksmith in town, a great greasy man with a bad reputation. Dad had told us not to hang around the blacksmith shop, so we spent as much time there as possible. We were dawdling around the shop and the shed he lived in, generally getting in his way, when we discovered something remarkable. He was resting on a dirty old mattress while we were boring him with talk; suddenly he yawned and dug his huge hands into the mattress in a finger-flexing grip.

To our amazement, the foot of the mattress curled upward from the sheer strength of his grip. As he gathered a handful of mattress where his hands rested near his waist, the whole mattress buckled and the end turned up.

Well, in no time at all, we had talked the smith into helping us. We covered him with a ragged blanket and someone ran to get Fred and tell him the blacksmith was possessed by the same spirit as the girl at McKinney. Sure enough, Fred came to the shed, along with several other boys. Curiosity had gotten the best of him.

As we gathered around the bed, the smith played along wonderfully.

"Oh, boys," he moaned, "That old spirit's got me!"

At that, under the blanket, he dug his enormous hands into the ticking and gripped for all he was worth. The whole foot end of the bed—blacksmith, blanket, and mattress—began to quiver and rise as if lifted by some invisible force.

Fred screamed and ran; we didn't see him for two weeks.

128 Ghost of Vengeance

The old people tell this to frighten and warn the young people:

From Yotsuya, in Tokyo, came a samurai warrior who married a beautiful lady named Oiwa. She was very faithful and attentive to him and only called him "Husband," in the old style, instead of by his name. So I do not know his name, but her name everyone from Japan knows. Her name was Oiwa.

Oiwa and Otto-san were very happy together at first, but with time the warrior's eyes began to fall on other women. He was especially pleased to meet Matsue, a younger woman from a great family. He began to resent Oiwa and plotted to free himself to marry Matsue. As he and Oiwa were walking home from a great banquet on the darkest night of the month, he pushed Oiwa over the cliffs into the bay.

At dawn, he and his friends combed the beach below and found the broken body of Oiwa with her face crushed and her hair full of seaweed. He claimed her fall was an accident. After the funeral, the warrior slept alone on the mat in his empty house, glad to be free of Oiwa, dreaming of Matsue.

Outside the wind blew, and the sliding paper walls of the room shook. Slowly, in the moonlight, one wall-door slid open. There stood Oiwa. Her long hair, so neatly arranged in life, hung loose about her shoulders; her beautiful kimono was gone; she wore a long white robe. Her face was ugly and dirty. Some of her teeth were missing. One eye hung out of its socket. Her arms were bony, like an old woman's. Her hands were like claws.

She said one word to Otto-san: "Vengeance."

The warrior screamed and ran from the house. The next night he slept in an abandoned house nearby, hoping the ghost could not find him. He awoke with a start at midnight. The single paper lantern he had left burning hung above his mat. Vines of ivy grew through a break in the wall. Slowly the vines began to writhe like snakes, and moved into the shape of Oiwa's body. The wind blew through a crack and the paper lantern swung. The candle inside guttered and the paper caught fire. The burned places on the lantern looked like eyes. The bottom of the burning lantern dropped away partially and flapped like a jaw talking, and two holes burned like eyes looked at the warrior.

"Vengeance," said the lantern.

The vines reached up at the warrior. The warrior cut his way through the vines with his sword and ran down the road screaming.

The next day at an inn, the warrior sat with two friends drinking tea. The steam was rising from the teapot. The steam became the shape of Oiwa. The two friends rose and drew their swords and tried to kill the warrior. When he shouted at them, "Why are you doing this?" it was Oiwa's voice that answered from their mouths.

"Vengeance."

The warrior ran out of the inn and looked back. The ghost of Oiwa was there. Her body stood at the doorway to the inn, and her neck grew longer and longer, so that her head followed him down the road. He drew his sword and cut off the head. It fell to the ground like a melon, then lay there and laughed at him.

The warrior prepared to marry Matsue. He persuaded her family to come and see his house and see how finely Matsue would live after they were married. When he and Matsue were alone in one room with Matsue behind a screen, Oiwa came and spoke to him. Matsue heard the woman's voice and thought that the warrior was seeing another woman. Matsue did not look out from behind the screen. Oiwa became more and more beautiful. Her eye went back into her socket. her broken teeth were restored, her hair was combed and neatly pinned up. She looked younger and younger. She came to Otto-san and she whispered in his ear.

"Vengeance," she whispered.

Matsue began not to trust the warrior and became jealous. He begged her to forgive him and marry him. He held a great feast for their intended engagement. All his friends and relatives came. Oiwa came, too.

The ghost came into the feast room and stood in the corner. The warrior tried to distract everyone with loud boasting and laughter; he did not know that only he could see her. Slowly, Oiwa's face began to grow larger and larger, filling the room. The warrior stumbled back out of its way, knocking over a table and tea service. His friends thought he was drunk. They could not see the hideous head with its loose eyeball and broken teeth, its seaweed-tangled hair and rotten skin, filling up the room.

The warrior began to rant and rave. He drew his sword and swung it at the head. His friends thought he was trying to kill them. They overpowered him and left in disgust. Matsue ran from the place, ashamed and frightened. All the guests laughed in scorn and disgust. Oiwa laughed, too.

The night was dark, as before. The moon was dark, as before. The warrior and Oiwa walked the path above the bay, as before. It was too late for regret or repentance; it was time for insanity and death.

"Vengeance," said the skull-face of the corpse.

The samurai warrior stepped off the cliff and was gone. Oiwa was gone, too.

129 *The Legend of Vivia*

There is a strange grave marker in the cemetery where my father is buried, in Fort Gibson, Oklahoma. In the Circle of Honor, there is the grave of the only woman ever to serve as a man in the cavalry.

Vivia Thomas had fallen in love with a young man back East, where they both lived. When he joined the Army and was sent west to Indian Territory, she followed him secretly, suspecting that he would not be faithful to her.

She dressed as a fair young man and enlisted in the same fort as her lover. No one recognized her as a woman, and he didn't recognize her since he would never have expected to see her there. She secretly followed him, and sure enough, she found that he was spending time at night in the home of a local girl even though he had been engaged to Vivia when he went West. She became enraged with a desire for revenge.

On a December night in 1869, she waited by the road near the local girl's home, and as her former lover rode by, she shot him with a rifle. Because the local girl was an Indian, the Army assumed that the Indians had killed the lieutenant to keep him away from the local girl.

No one would have ever suspected, except for the fact that Vivia began to see the dead lieutenant's ghost, visiting her each night, filling her with grief and remorse. She confessed the killing to a chaplain, and began to go nightly to sit at her dead lover's grave and cry. She froze to death on January 7, 1870, a victim of the bitter cold, of bitter remorse, and of the visitations of the ghost of her former lover, murdered by her own hand.

130 *Hand of Time*

Years ago, my family and I lived in Prescott [Arizona] and I worked at the Yavapai County fairground. I drove a blade grader between the horse barns whenever it got muddy or churned up. When the ground firmed up some, I bladed it smooth again. The fairground sits on an ancient Indian burial ground; pottery shards and arrowheads have been found there for over a century.

One February, after a three-inch snow had melted, I began to blade when something caught my eye: a piece of pottery with black-and-white designs, upright and intact in the mud.

I climbed off the grader and dug up with my bare hands three pots, a perfect spearhead, and a piece of basalt rock. When I touched a human jawbone with teeth, a chill went through me, and I filled the hole back in.

At home, I soaked the muddy artifacts in a basin. The next morning, I was stunned to see the water in the basin blood red in color. As the water drained out, I found red pigment in one bowl and ash-white in another. The artifacts were put on display on a shelf in the den, to show to friends when they came over.

Within a week, I was laid off from my job and my wife began to have nightmares. In a month, the car was repossessed. Our family life took a turn for the worse. My wife blamed the artifacts, but I didn't believe her. Finally, she said either the artifacts had to go or she would have to go to get away from them.

Late on a Tuesday night, I climbed the fence to the fairground, crept back between the barns with a hand-spade, and dug a hole near where I had been before. I buried the artifacts deep in the earth.

As I drove away from the fairground and stopped for a red light, my old boss pulled up beside me and said that the board of directors had come up with some money and would I like my old job back.

We got caught up on our bills, and everything went back to normal in our lives, untouched by the hand of time.

One night that May, we put our daughter to bed, but she came walking into the den a few hours later, crying.

"What's the matter," I asked, "are you sick?"

"My friend went away," she said, shaking her head.

"All your friends are still here," I said. "Nobody's moved away."

"No," she said, "the old man is gone."

"What old man?" I asked.

"The old Indian man. His face was painted red and white. He used to sit at the end of the bed and sing to me."

I hadn't an answer for that. Only goosebumps.

131   *The Legend of Polly*

In 1867, Ephraim Polly came to Fort Hays, Kansas, with his wife Elizabeth. There was a great cholera epidemic, and Elizabeth worked to help the sick and dying. She finally took the fever and died. She was buried in a lonely grave on the prairie.

Years later, a woman in old-fashioned clothing was seen walking among the outbuildings and empty barns near the gravesite. She was dressed in a plain light blue dress. No one knew who she was, and no one ever got near her. She would go around a corner and just vanish.

Some people called the woman "Polly," but that was her last name. It's Elizabeth, Elizabeth Polly, still tending the sick and dying, who alone can see her spirit.

132 *La Llorona at Yuma*

There were men coming in from Spain who married Indian women in Mexico. And at that time there was a Spanish soldier who married an Indian girl by common-law. They were very much in love and had two children. And at that time if you were married by common-law you couldn't have any inheritance or rights to good jobs. You had to be married to a Spanish woman. So, he legally married a Spanish woman who came by ship from Spain. The Indian woman became angry, bitter, and jealous over the man having left her. She became temporarily insane, and she drowned her two children to get revenge. Later she came to her senses and regretted that she had drowned them. She then actually became insane after realizing what she did. She was cursed to forever roam Mexico where there was a body of water to look for her children. And because of the sadness she wails a long sad cry. And to this day perople say you can hear her wail, looking for her children. She is cursed to do this forever for what she did.

[The motif of passing into, out of, and back into insanity makes this variant unusual, and resembles the plotline of stories about insanity caused by the vision of the ghosts of the victims.]

Lifestyles of the Dead and Famous

133 Lafffite's Treasure at LaPorte

Once there stood in the town of Laporte an old house haunted by the ghost of Jean Laffite. The house sat facing Trinity Bay, which opens into the Gulf of Mexico at Galveston Island in Texas. More than once, someone tried to seek shelter in the old abandoned structure. Each one was awakened in the middle of the night, usually during a wind storm, by a ghostly figure that hovered near his sleeping place.

It is Laffite, the pirate of the Gulf, the lord of Galveston, dressed in a red coat and breeches. It points to the place beneath the floor where, in life, it buried treasure long before the house was built.

"Take the treasure. It is mine to give you. I earned it with the forfeiture of my immortal soul."

The ghost fixes the traveller with its sad gaze.

"But the money must all be spent in charity. Not one penny may you spend in evil or in selfishness. What was taken in selfishness and evil must be spent for good."

The ghost vanishes in the sudden light of a lightning flash in the storm outside. The traveller seldom sleeps again that night. And no one has ever touched the treasure, Laffite's treasure at LaPorte.

134 *Petit Jean*

High above the Arkansas River stands Petit Jean Mountain. On its southeast overlook is a tiny grave surrounded by a rusting iron fence. People who live in the valley below often see lights hovering around the grave late, late at night. Some say it's just kids or tourists; the rest know it's what the Indians saw for years before the valley was settled. It's the ghost of Petit Jean.

When the French explorer Cheves set sail from France to come to the New World, he left behind his fiancée, Adrienne, in the town of Calais. Just before he sailed, a new cabin boy signed on, a youth with a lovely face. The boy followed the troupe up the Mississippi and up the Arkansas. When the explorers reached the escarpment above the present town of Morrilton, they stopped.

A little settlement was built with log houses, and the friendly Indians of the area were fascinated with the mysterious boy. They saw in him features of both man and woman, and considered this to be a sign of spiritual gifts. His name was Jean, called "Little."

When Cheves announced that he would return to France and bring his fiancée back to this pleasant land, the cabin boy asked to go, too. When Cheves refused, the lad fell very ill. The Indians cared for the lad and learned the strange truth. They told Cheves that the cabin boy was Adrienne, who had followed him in disguise.

Cheves rushed to her side, but she died in his arms, telling him that she loved him and this place and these Indian people. She was buried atop the escarpment, and her ghost walks the cliff edge still as the beautiful Little John—our Petit Jean.

135 *Marie Laveau*

They who believe in voudou come to the St. Louis Cemetery on moonless nights, and by candlelight, they see the ghost of

Marie Laveau passing forth and back between the Two Worlds, carrying blessing or curse to those who believe or do not believe.

In life, she danced in Congo Square and sold potions and charms from the house at 1020 Ste. Anne Street. They see her ghost there, too. She comes all dressed in white, sometimes with a snake for a necklace.

She was killed in the hurricane of 1890, but she was reborn from her open grave before it could be closed. Then she lived long years and died again. She is a good ghost to those who believe.

136 Kit Carson's Ghost

Kit Carson's wife and Governor Bent's wife were sisters. The Carson home sits about two hundred yards from the Bents' home. Both are now museums. Both families named a daughter Maria. Both houses are said to be haunted.

Kit Carson's wife was a very pretty lady. Most of the Hispanic women here in Taos were very short of stature. All of my family [the receptionist's] are of short stature, and we were some of the first settlers to come to Taos directly from Spain, following the Old Santa Fe Trail. My family settled in a district that is now designated a historic district; my great-grandfather donated the land that the Chapel of St. Anthony now stands on and got permission from the king of Spain to dedicate the chapel to St. Anthony.

Much of Taos is the same today as it was in Kit Carson's time, and his house here is very well-preserved. It started out with just the three rooms facing the road; then they built these rooms back here for their children. The descendants come around to visit the museum, but the ancestors are here, too. Kit Carson is still here, his spirit. He's in the house. If you are sentimental, or nostalgic, or whatever you want to call it, you can feel his presence. I do.

It's a good feeling, because I've never been afraid of his ghost; I've never been afraid.

137 The Ghostly Mob

Governor Bent of Taos was killed January 18, 1847. An angry mob had gathered around his residence just off the Plaza to protest American rule, enforced in the Mexican War. Governor Bent went out bravely and tried to reason with them. They shot him with bullets, shot him with arrows. Indian men came forward and scalped him.

Inside, his family escaped by burrowing through the two-foot-thick adobe walls into the house next door, and the neighbors let them go out a back door.

The men who killed Bent were eventually caught, tried, and hanged. It's not Bent that haunts the house, it's the ghostly mob, the ghosts of the hanged men, that come back and can be faintly seen or heard at night some still nights.

138 Father Juan Padilla's Coffin

Father Juan Padilla served the mission at Laguna Pueblo in 1733. He was murdered, some say by a Spaniard, others say by Indians who had renounced Christianity. He was buried beneath the floor of the church at Isleta Pueblo where his horse had carried the murdered priest. His spirit, indeed his very body, did not rest in the grave. The coffin in which he was buried, hollowed from a cottonwood log, rose back out of the earth in front of the altar and was reburied.

It rose again, almost twenty years later, in response to the prayers of the Indian believers in time of famine or epidemic, or in response to Indian dances, which are also prayers, held inside the church. An investigation was held in 1819, and another one after the coffin rose in 1889, after a *Noche Buena* [Christmas Eve] dance. Ordered by the bishops at Santa Fe, the investigations never found an explanation for the periodic reappearance of the coffin and its ghostly contents.

The coffin rose for the last known time Christmas Eve in 1914, as the world went to war.

Geologists suggest that shifting sand in the soil accounts for the coffin rising. The inhabitants know better. It is the ghost of Father Padilla, who does not rest well, returning to the world of those awake.

139 Howling Ghosts of Goliad

General Santa Ana [the Mexican dictator] was captured after the battle of San Jacinto [Texas] and taken to Velasco at the mouth of the Brazos River. He was needed alive to enforce the treaty he had signed. [If he were executed in Texas, a subsequent Mexican ruler might renounce the treaty.] To protect Santa Ana from Texans seeking vengeance for [the massacre at] Goliad, he was imprisoned at the Patton Plantation (later the Hogg Plantation) near old Columbia, the first capital of the Republic of Texas.

Later, to prevent discovery by loyalists or escape attempts by Santa Ana himself, he was moved to Orozimbo Plantation until December of 1836. Despite the move and attempts at total secrecy, Mexican loyalists living in Texas found out and crept toward Orozimbo by night to attempt a rescue of their President. They were driven away in fear by the unearthly baying of hounds in the trees near the plantation. The loyalists fled and never returned.

This alone would not prove strange, but Orozimbo had no dogs. Nor were there any strays known to be in the trees at the time of the rescue attempt.

Guards at Orozimbo who heard the howling had an explanation: The baying was not hounds, but the hellish cry of ghosts—the ghosts of the victims of the Goliad massacre.

Only very rarely, and not at all in the last few decades, visitors to Orozimbo claim to have heard the howls.

The howling of the ghosts from Goliad.

140 The Ghost at Chrétienne Point

Chrétienne Point mansion in Louisiana was the inspiration for the interior sets of Tara in *Gone With The Wind*. In fact, the grand staircase at Chrétienne Point is copied exactly in the scene where Rhett carries Scarlett up the steps, but the scene is reversed, with the windows on the opposite side from where they really are. The story goes that the set designer took a picture at Chrétienne Point and the negative was printed backwards.

Madame Chrétienne was a wild woman, long ago. She had lived with her husband's gambling all their married life, and after he was killed over a gambling disagreement, she turned into the wildest woman of her day. She gambled, smoked, drank, and carried on in a way unknown among ladies at the time. She turned her mansion into a gaming house and would join the men with a drink and a box of cigars, and sit and gamble all night. Her Negro servant would pass among the guests serving drinks, and he gave her winks and nods that told her what her opponents held during the card games.

Jean Laffite and his crew were good friends of Madame Chrétienne and would often come to drink and gamble at the Point. After Laffite's death, his men became renegades and turned from organized privateering to plain burglary. They came one night and tried to break in to the Point, but the house was well locked after closing time. They knew she was quite rich, and where the wealth was kept, so they broke down the door.

Hearing them outside the mansion, Madame Chrétienne had gathered all her belongings—her money, her jewelry, her gold, everything she had that was of value. She had thrown it into her long dress and held it up from the hem making her dress a long bag. She was in the act of escaping, with her dress up and her hoops showing, when the doorframe gave way and a pirate entered the front hall and stopped her at the head of the grand staircase.

"Stop, Madame," he called out, aiming his single-shot pistol at her, "and throw down the money you have in your dress!"

She stood up proudly and dropped the front of her dress. Money, jewels, and gold cascaded down the grand staircase, tumbling and rolling toward the astounded pirate.

As he dropped to his knees to grab the first coins to reach the hardwood floor, she drew her small hidden pistol and said, "Excuse me..."

When he looked up, she shot him square between the eyes. His blood stained the stairs and cannot be scrubbed away. If there were others with the pirate, they fled at the sound of gunfire. Madame Chrétienne stuffed the body into a closet and left it three days until the sheriff could be reached.

Today, the ghost of Madame Chrétienne walks the mansion, and one can hear the pistol shot, the fatal blow to the skull as the ball strikes the pirate, and the sound of the pirate's body striking the floor or rolling loudly down the bottommost steps.

Those who manage the mansion today do not relate the final point of the legend: not only will the pirate's bloodstains not scrub away, but when the ghost of the Madame walks by night, the bloodstains again reliquify. The steps are now carpeted, but those who know the whole legend say that the blood boils up even underneath the carpet.

141   *The Ghost of Lunt Mansion*

I work at a restaurant in St. Louis that was once listed by *LIFE Magazine* as being one of the three most haunted houses in the United States. It's the famous Lunt Mansion.

There were four suicides in the mansion in its heyday, and that's the source of the ghostly happenings there. My mother works in the kitchen and she has many times heard someone calling her name when she was all alone in the kitchen, and no one outside the kitchen said they had called her.

The most spectacular suicide, as I recall, was in 1949, when Charles Lunt led the family dog to the upstairs attic landing and shot it and then himself. When television crews came in one time, I'm told, the only sound they could get on tape was the barking of the ghost dog.

Mother also says that sometimes pans will rattle by themselves. She can be looking directly at them, and they shake on their hooks and rattle and almost fall from the rack.

The mansion originally belonged to the Falstaff Brewery owners and is just up the street from the Budweiser Beer family mansion. The recent owner of the restaurant stayed at the home one night after some vandalism had been done. He heard a large commotion, and he began to work his way through the mansion looking for a source of noise. All the doors were locked from the inside, but the doors inside the mansion were all standing open, as they do during business hours. As the owner came to one entryway, the two heavy wooden doors slammed shut in front of him with no visible cause.

The main source of the haunting is the ghost of Charles Lunt. He is not buried in the family mausoleum and his ghost still walks his old home, to the delight of restaurant-goers who enjoy the atmosphere.

142 *They're Still Home*

Tony Luján was a Taos Pueblo Indian; he married Mabel Dodge after a divorce. They built a beautiful home and a small adobe house on Tony's land—Indian land. Years after both these prominent members of Taos society had died, actor Dennis Hopper bought the house.

He saw these phantasms—it was in all the newspapers in the mid-70s—just the upper half of the Lujáns, from the waist up, floating in one room of the house, laughing.

His wife saw Mabel once, just a vaporous emanation, moving through the hallway near a bathroom, going right through the walls.

Collection Notes

These collection notes are provided to give proper credit to informants and sources and to answer some of the reader's questions about the background or origin of a given story. These notes do not provide all the data a folklorist would wish or would have obtained at the time of collection. Many of the stories have come from the repertories of the editors themselves, and many were collected before this anthology was planned. Often notes are very brief or tellers described as "unidentified"; these and other stories labelled "collected before January 1, 1989," are from that pre-anthology period. In other cases, notes are very brief or tellers listed as "anonymous" at the request of the teller.

Notes may begin with any of the following phrases:

Collected by... indicates that another storyteller or a folklorist obtained this narrative and passed it along to the editors.

Collected from... means that we obtained this narrative ourselves, directly and orally, from the listed informant or source, or from the listed informant and others not listed specifically.

Learned from... refers to stories in the repertories of the editors that we have told for years.

Provided by... indicates that the listed source or informant was the primary source of fragmentary material or wrote the story down for us (usually transmitting it to us by mail) when oral collection was not feasible.

Retold from... refers to a story we heard from another storyteller and are passing along to the reader. Some unconscious addition or deletion may exist in our variant of the story in as much as all storytellers are likely to alter a story slightly with their own telling style, even when it is not their intention to do so.

Numbers refer to the number of the story, not the page number.

1. This ghost joke exists in many variants in the South and Southwest. This version was learned from Lewin Hayden Dockrey in Wagoner, Oklahoma, in the 1950s. The father of Judy Dockrey Young, and the man to whose memory this collection is dedicated, Mr. Dockrey told this as his favorite ghost story, even though no ghosts or spirits appear therein.

2. Learned from Homer Harry Young, Ph.D., in the 1950s. Sometimes known as "You Can't Get Out," this ghost joke is also very well-known throughout the South and Southwest. Dr. Young was the uncle of Richard Alan Young, and the source of much of this editor's love of ghost stories.

3. Collected anonymously from a teen-aged boy in Harrison, Arkansas, prior to January 1, 1989. The young man swears the grandfather told the story as the truth. The "victim" who saw the skeleton had long since died or the boy would have sought him out for more information. The young man called this story "I Can't Get In."

4. Learned from the Rev. John Morgan Young, a Baptist preacher in Dallas, Texas, in the early 1950s. After the Rev. Young's death in 1957, his son Morgan Martin Young, Ed.D., also told the story. Richard Alan Young heard it from both grandfather and father, although the former called the car a "darn thing."

5. This tongue-in-cheek story was submitted anonymously for this collection as "A Ghost Story for Folklorists." It is constructed of folktale motif numbers used to classify traditional narratives. It is a well-known "ghost joke," and reads, approximately, thus:

    "Once, on a dare to prove his bravery, a young man spent the night in a graveyard. He fell asleep, and at midnight the ghosts of the dead [were] in the graveyard and suddenly [the] ghosts awaken [the] sleeper. The young man jumped up and saw ghostly lights all around him and heard the voices of the dead conversing in the graveyard!

    Up from behind a huge tombstone [a] coffin moves by itself and it [object] floats in [the] air toward him.

    "He began to run, and it chased him as [object behaves as] if [it were] alive!

    "He ran all around the graveyard and finally took a cough drop and stopped the coffin [that] moves by itself."

    The pun of *coffin* on *coughin'* works best, of course, when said aloud. Since the motif numbers are phrases instead of clauses, the

grammar of this waggish tale has been both added to and sub-
tracted from with the words in brackets. Our apologies to the
folklorists among our readers, but this unique tale was too good
(or too bad) to pass up.

6. "The Skin and Bones Woman" as sung by Lillian Deaver Sears,
1887-1973, learned in childhood at Elm Springs (Washington
County), Arkansas, by her daughter JoAnne Sears Rife. Passed
along to the editors March 13, 1990. This song and others of its
type, wherein young listeners are frightened at the end, are a
common Hallowe'en practice in the Ozarks.

7. The most famous of the American urban legends, this story is
often called "The Vanishing Hitchhiker," and is told in hundreds
of variants in every state in the Union. This version is sometimes
called "Last Kiss," the name by which the editors of this collection
first heard it in Texas in the 1950s. Other elements sometimes
included are: the boy sees a photograph in the dead girl's home
for positive identification, the girl has been brought home by a
different boy each year for many years, or the mother accuses the
boy of making a cruel joke in claiming to have seen the daughter.
Jan Harold Brunvand's *The Vanishing Hitchhiker* gives this legend
well-deserved attention and presents innumerable variants on it.
Learned in adolescence by the editors, this version comes from
many informants and sources in Texas and Oklahoma.

8. Jean Laffite (his own spelling) never wore a hook, and although
he privateered off Barataria Island south of New Orleans, there is
no reason to associate him with this story, which is usually named
"Hook-Arm" or "The Hook Man" and is one of the most popular
urban legends of this century. This version was contributed by
teenagers from Louisiana prior to 1989.

9. This is a well-known urban legend, told in California and in
Oklahoma, where it is purported to have come back home with
returning workers who had fled to California during the Dust
Bowl. The legend entered the editor's collection long ago, and
has been heard by them in many variants, including a recent
telling by California storytellers at the National Storytelling Fes-
tival in October, 1990, in Jonesborough, Tennessee.

10. Homer Harry Young, Ph.D., was a professor of education at Rice
Institute and later Rice University in the 1950s and 1960s. Since
Rice had no summer school for education, he taught summers at
Texas Southern University, Bishop College, or Paul Quinn College. From teachers and students in summer school he collected
folk tales or urban legends. While there were no collection notes
among his papers at the time of his death in 1967, he passed many
stories along to his brother Morgan Martin Young, Ed.D., and his
nephew Richard Alan Young, one of the editors of this collec-

tion.This story is from the Waco, Texas, area, and is a variant on the classic English folktale "Golden Arm." This variant is sometimes called "Pair of Pants."

11. This complex scary story is told in many variants throughout the Southwest, especially at Girl Scout and Boy Scout camps. Heard from numerous tellers since 1963, our version is based on the tellings of Scott Doss of Dallas, Texas, and Carl Christofferson, formerly of Hillsboro, Missouri. Although this version has no ghost, some variants tell of the headless ghost tormenting one or more members of the team until they commit suicide. The story often ends with the teller screaming or jumping at the audience; experienced campers move slowly to the rear during the telling, putting the "greenhorns" who've never heard it up front for the ending. Other camps use it as the last story of the evening to try to insure nightmares or at least very nervous latrine trips afterward. The story has numerous names but seems to be most often known as "The Freshman Initiation."

12. Learned from Bobby Dahms of Whittier, California, in 1967. Mr. Dahms had heard it in California and tells it purely for entertainment. This urban legend is well-known throughout the South and Southwest and is usually known by the name "Call from the Grave."

13. Collected numerous times in variants from adults and teenagers over the ten-year period 1980-1990. This variant is largely that of Tom Phillips of Edmond, Oklahoma. Mr. Phillips and many others we have talked to point out that for some reason, one does begin to notice 11:11 more often after hearing the story. The phenomenon persists for a very long time, perhaps indefinitely. Mr. Phillips suggests that you see different times on a digital clock readout and don't "remember" or "notice" the odd times like 1:27 or 3:52; but since there's a story about it, you "notice" and remember noticing it when the time reads 11:11. In some versions of the story, the time is given as 1:11. The editors suggest that this reflects a later curfew for kids in the 90s than in the 70s and 80s. The older versions also have the clock in the car stopping at the time of the wreck at 11:11, but battery-operated digital clocks don't "stop"; they just flash 12:00 over and over and over. This variant was collected August 6, 1990, in Edmond.

14. Collected from a young Hispanic man in his 20s in Santa Fe, New Mexico, in December of 1987. He firmly believed the story to be true, and "sightings" of The Weeping Woman (or "The Wailing Woman") are common among the Hispanos of New Mexico and Arizona. *La LLorona* is the "Bogey Woman" of the Southwest, either warning miscreants to change their lives or visiting retribution on wrongdoers who persist in their sins (or

who have ignored her previous warnings). She appears most often to children and drunkards (who are, after all, childlike when intoxicated), but is also seen by others. She usually appears as a woman dressed in black, although she also dresses in white. She often appears first as a young woman and then changes to a hag (although she has also been seen to appear young and simply vanish, appear old and simply vanish, appear young and turn to a skeleton, or appear old and turn to a skeleton). *La LLorona* seems to be a purely Mexican and Mexican- American phenomenon, based on an Aztec mythological character. Various authorities suggest she is Civacoatl (Cihuacoatl), Tonantzín or Coatlicue. As Coatlicue, she would be a bogey woman; as Civacoatl (also called Tlillan, or Blackness), she would call for sacrifices by carrying a basket-cradle containing a stone knife instead of a baby and leaving it with some unsuspecting woman in the marketplace. Another possibility is that *la LLorona* is one of the Cihuapipiltin (Mothers-of-children-who-died-in-first-childbirth). They came to earth one night a year to cry for the loss of their dead children. They often haunted crossroads and were often associated with the *ignis fatuus,* or fool's fire. *See stories numbers 44 and 45, and the Introduction for more about* la LLorona.

15. Collected in the winter of 1967 from the late Michael Olin Poe, who saw the light as a teen-ager from Sheridan, Arkansas. The light appears near the town of Crossett, Arkansas, in Ashley County. Residents from there and nearby Hamburg claim the light has been seen for at least half a century and is still seen as of this writing. Poe died in the line of duty as a policeman in Texas, and this story is a fond memento for the collectors of this anthology. The same narrative explanation is given for other ghost-lights or "spooklights," including one seen along the tracks at nearby Gurdon, Arkansas, and in other states as well.

16. Collected from Sean Bishop of Altus, Oklahoma, on June 25, 1990. *See the note to story number 79.*

17. Collected from Tom Phillips of Edmond, Oklahoma, on August 5, 1990. Mr. Phillips, in his 30s, relates an experience from his college days and suggests that the New Madrid Fault near the site may somehow be the cause of the lights.

18. Collected by Tom Phillips *(see note above)* from college pal Bobby Box, in Jonesboro, Arkansas, in the 1970s, this story/event was passed along with a laugh to the editors on August 6, 1990. This narrative is an excellent example of how a hoax may enter folklore to the frustration of serious storyholders or folklorists. Mr. Phillips swears he knew other college students who "fell" for the story and the hoax event, never bothering to look at the radio tower or make the mental connection.

19. Retold from a teen-aged girl's account in Siloam Springs, Arkansas, in 1962. She requested anonymity at that time. This is the only instance the editors know of this phenomenon being reported as ball lightning.

20. Learned from Jimmy Carter on October 18, 1990. Mr. Carter resides in Kansas, but the events of this story took place in Nebraska. Mr. Carter tells this family narrative as the truth. Mr. Carter assumes that the explanation is ball lightning. The association of the ball of fire with a bridge over a river follows the general belief that ball lightning follows "conductive material" (e.g., water, railroad tracks, etc.) as it moves along above the earth. Mr. Carter's grandfather was Joseph Augustine Wright.

21. Collected from an anonymous informant whose employers indicate that this story is not to be spread. The editors regret presenting such a fascinating story with the deletions and lack of annotation, but this is what the informant requested. The informant is a white male Emergency Medical Technician in his 20s, and he believes the story to be the truth.

22. Retold from Dr. H. H. Young, who collected it in the 1960s in central Texas from black educators studying in summer school. *See also the note for story number 10.*

23. Collected from Terry Bloodworth of Kimberling City, Missouri, in October, 1990. Mr. Bloodworth saw the light near Texarkana, Arkansas, personally, as described in the narrative. Mr. Bloodworth is a fine storyteller and has contributed many stories to this collection.

24. Provided by two informants from East Texas prior to January 1, 1989.

25. Collected from Katie Wamser of the Miami area during July of 1989. Ms. Wamser has seen the light and accepts its ghostly nature as the truth. Some other informants suggest the light is caused somehow by the nearby mining operations. The Hornet spooklight is only about thirty miles away in southwestern Missouri, and both lights might have the same explanation.

26. Retold from a dozen Missouri informants during 1989 and 1990. This is the "standard" folkloric explanation for the Hornet light.

27. Collected from Johnny Brewer from Grove, Oklahoma, (just across the state line from the Hornet spooklight) in August of 1989. Mr. Brewer did not accept the explanation, but found the story fascinating.

28. Collected in October, 1990, at Silver Dollar City from Betty Gresham, a resident of Stone County, Missouri.

29. Collected in August, 1989, at Silver Dollar City from Bill Frenchman, a resident of Disney, Oklahoma.

30. Provided by more than one informant from West Texas between 1957 and 1985. This well-known story has several conflicting versions, depending on the ending (which seems to depend on the general outlook of the teller). Some authorities give *chisos* as the Apache word for ghost, but it is more likely a corruption of *hechicero* (sorceror) in Spanish.

31. Collected from Louis Darby, of Opelousas, Louisiana, in August of 1989.

32. Provided by John H. Snow, of Texas A. & M. University, College Station, Texas. Collected in 1989 from a freshman student of Mrs. Amma Davis of Sam Houston State University. There are many explanations for the Marfa Lights, but this is a variant of the most commonly accepted story. Other legends involving Indian chiefs and warriors are almost certainly romanticized fictions invented in this century.

    The Marfa Lights came into new prominence when the NBC television series *Unsolved Mysteries* featured them in one episode. Videotapes of the Marfa Lights, like those taken of the Hornet Light by NBC affiliate KYTV in Springfield, Missouri, are faint and inconclusive.

    Mr. Snow identifies two types of ghost lights: some, like the Marfa Lights, are thought of by local people as being simply lights; others, like the ghost lights at Stampede Mesa, are thought of as being ghosts.

33. Collected from Bill Frenchman, of Disney, Oklahoma, in August of 1989. Mr. Frenchman offers no explanation for the lights, but other tellers have alluded to the ghosts of miners in their hard hats with lanterns. The miners in such explanatory stories have always been victims of a cave-in or explosion, never having died from natural causes.

34. Provided by an anonymous informant in Albuquerque, New Mexico, in January, 1990. The story is also told of the Río Puerco area below El Cabezón. *See stories number 80 and 81.*

35. Collected from an anonymous informant in Albuquerque, New Mexico, in January, 1990. There are many stories about *braseros* (fireball, brazier, fire-pan) in the Río Puerco area. Numerous first-person narratives appear in *Recuerdos de los Viejitos: Tales of the Río Puerco,* collected and edited by Nasario García, published by the University of New Mexico Press, Albuquerque. These first-person narratives appear to be passing in and out of the oral tradition as they are retold by people who read them, as well as being told by people who heard them in their original oral form. It is impossible to tell which source any given narrative has. Many explanations are offered for the fireball phenomenon, ranging from the igniting of sulphurous gas near El Cabezón to the work

of *brujos* (sorcerers). This type of narrative is a favorite in the Albuquerque area and is told with both great animation and complete belief.

36. Learned from numerous sources over the twenty years we have collected in the Ozarks, this is the most popular scary story in northern Arkansas and southern Missouri. It is known by names such as "Old Raw Head," "Raw Head and Bloody Bones," and "Bloody Bones and Rawhide." This variant contains the most prevalent motifs and represents the best tellings we have encountered. Technically, the Old Raw Head is a preternatural creature, not a ghost, but the implication that it is alive through conjuring (similar to witchcraft) places it into the Southwestern concept of ghost lore and witch lore being interchangeable.

37. Provided by a man in San Antonio who is a member of the Sons of Confederate Veterans. He declined to be identified and suggested that we seek out written sources. Sightings of the Confederate bridge guard were more common in the 1930s and '40s. The informant speculated that the bridge was either replaced by a new one or that the presence of Interstate 10 nearby had caused sightings to cease.

38. The White Wolf is a common theme in folk narratives; any animal albinism may be. There was a well-known white wolf in Montana in 1915, and there must have been many others in the West over the centuries. The white wolf story may be an offshoot of the Pecos Bill fantasy or of the Wolf Girl of Devil's River *(see story number 103)*, or it may be nothing more than a romanticization of an albino wolf sighting. This narrative was collected in Abilene, Texas, in 1958, from Otis Johnson, who was a lad of eleven at the time. There is no historical connection between the name of Fort Phantom Hill and the events of this story.

39. Learned in 1988 from an unidentified white male California truck driver in his 60s who had seen the ghostly event. Later confirmed in a variant provided by Bill Frenchman of Disney, Oklahoma, who had also seen personally the "Ghostly Battle." Mr. Frenchman provided us with his variant in August, 1990.

40. Collected by New Mexico storyteller Teresa Pijoan de Van Etten from various informants in the Santa Fe area and provided to these editors on December 31, 1989. The story has many variants that reflect the ethnic origin of the informant. In another version, published in her book *Spanish-American Folktales* (August House, Little Rock, 1990), Sra. de Van Etten attributes sightings or hearings of the severed head to fiesta time in September, as would accord with Hispanic tradition; in the version provided to us, the head is seen or heard around Hallowe'en, as related by the Anglos

living in Santa Fe. This story is the best known and most often repeated ghost story of Santa Fe.

41. Collected in the main library in Santa Fe from a patron who had heard the editors perform storytelling. Additional fragmentary information was provided by Kathy Costa of Oliver LaFarge Library in Santa Fe, all in December, 1989. When the editors asked Sr. Luján if he knew such a story, he said that he did not.

42. Collected from one of the museum guards at the Museum of Fine Arts in Santa Fe, in December, 1987, during the *la LLorona* exhibit there. The same Hispanic man in his 50s provided story number 45.

43. The stories of the Ghost Girl of the Mimbres were reported in local newspapers in 1906 and thereafter; the legend itself seems much older. Learned from unidentified New Mexicans before 1988. The expression "on the Mimbres" refers to the Mimbres Mountains that sweep down from the Continental Divide.

44. Collected from Sra. de Kraul while at El Ropero, a fine artesania shop in Santa Fe in late December, 1987. The Kraul and Garcia families have worked to promote *la LLorona* as the true Hispanic folk character for the Santa Fe area. At The Word Process (P.O. Box 5699, Santa Fe, NM 87502), they have published a book of stories called *La LLorona: Encounters with the Weeping Woman*.

45. Collected from a museum guard at the Museum of Fine Arts in Santa Fe in December, 1987, during the *la LLorona* exhibit there. He also provided story number 42.

46. Collected from Teresa Pijoan de Van Etten on December 31, 1989. Sra. de Van Etten has heard the story and its attendant warnings to young girls not to drive alone in the area at night all her life.

47. Learned from Dr. H. H. Young in the 1960s; he heard it from students at Paul Quinn College in Waco, Texas. Although the black educators who shared this story did not believe it to be true, they readily passed it on as area folklore.

48. Learned from various Texas sources prior to January 1, 1989. The stories of "Bigfoot" Wallace are numerous and well-known. Some locals regard him as a half-legendary, half-real folk character to rival Davy Crockett.

49. Collected in passing from a young white male in his 20s in downtown Wichita, Kansas, November 25, 1990. He told the fragment as if he had heard it and did not believe it to be true. He did not remember there being any more to the narrative.

50. Retold by Texas folklorist George D. Hendricks, of Denton, from a story originally collected by Mary E. Hill, of Dallas, and appeared (in different form) in Mr. Hendricks's *Mirrors, Mice, & Moustaches* (S.M.U. Press, Dallas, 1966). This story has many variants but

appears different from the "Vanishing Hitchhiker" story in that no one in this story recognized the ghost-girl. Other tellers have alluded to a spooklight associated with the White Rock Lady.

51a. The most famous ghost story from San Antonio, Texas. Originally collected from hearing-impaired students. *See note following.*

51b. Collected from Connie High on April 17, 1989, in San Antonio, Texas. At that time High was an intern at the Southwest Center for the Hearing Impaired. Sidney Brooks died Tuesday, November 13, 1917, on a training flight, and was one of the first cadet casualties in the new Army Air Corps. This story may appeal to the hearing-impaired because it deals with smell instead of sound. Using the descriptive technique of presenting the story in sign language was done to make it possible to recreate the story to deaf audiences exactly as it came to the collectors of this anthology.

52. Collected prior to January 1, 1989, anonymously from a teenager in Harrison, Arkansas (who is not the source of any other story in this anthology). It seems that most of the good ghost stories told in that part of north Arkansas are set in Newton County, a sparsely inhabited mountainous region where old oral traditions are kept.

53. Collected August 5, 1990, from storyteller Tom Phillips in Edmond, Oklahoma. Mr. Phillips works at Oklahoma Christian College and has gathered and told scary stories from college students since his own college days in the 70s. He does not claim that any of his stories are true; he doesn't deny that they are, either. He does state that he knew these brothers personally, and gave the family name, which the editors have declined to print.

54. Collected at Hallowe'en, 1971, from Henry A. Klussman, a free-lance writer from Houston, Texas, and the descendant of the girl in the story. In the Klussman family, the story is accepted as the truth.

55. Learned in the 1950s from the Rev. John Morgan Young, then of Dallas, Texas, and as retold by his sons Dr. H. H. Young and Dr. Morgan M. Young. The church was in Howe, Texas, but the Rev. Young's memory was unclear as to whether the house was in Howe or nearby Anna.

56. Collected from Teresa Pijoan de Van Etten in Placitas, New Mexico, December 31, 1989. The story of the Healing Lady of Los Luceros is the third in a trilogy of stories consisting of stories numbers 80, 81 and 56. Sra. de Van Etten personally knew occupants of the house in the last few decades. This story was told to Sra. de Van Etten by grnadmother Monelle Holley, now of Plano, Texas, to whom the story is considered to belong.

57. Learned from California residents prior to January 1, 1989. Various visitors to Silver Dollar City have shared versions with the editors in recent years.

58. Collected from Patricia Smith, June 11, 1990. Mrs. Smith lived for a time in California and saw the ghost of Helen at the home of relatives. Various family names have been omitted from the story out of respect for living members of families involved. When the editors ask for ghost stories, expecting to get folktales, we often receive first-person narratives like this, which are fascinating.

59. Collected from Janet Shaw on June 11, 1990, in Harrison, Arkansas. Mrs. Shaw had only recently moved from the house in nearby Alpena, Arkansas, where "the ghost played pool."

60. Collected from Scott Denning, who had heard the story from Valerie Money, whose family had bought the house in the story. Mr. Denning provided the story to the editors at the Chile Hill Emporium in Bernalillo, New Mexico, in December, 1989.

61. Provided by Mary Grathwol, a librarian with the Library Storytellers of Santa Fe, New Mexico, in December, 1989.

62. Collected from Teri Murguía, from San Francisco, California, on July 26, 1989, when she was in Branson, Missouri. Certain family names were omitted at her request.

63. Collected from Terry Bloodworth of Kimberling City, Missouri, in August of 1990. The "House on Chalet Road" is in Hollister, Missouri, near Lake Taneycomo. Mr. Bloodworth's work as a glassblower does not interfere with his hobby as a fine storyteller.

64. Collected from George Wamser in July of 1989. Mr. Wamser lives in Oklahoma now, but his family lived in El Monte, California. The ghost in the house in the story is unusual in that it possesses or causes an aroma. *See also story number 51.*

65. Collected from Terryl Hébert of Kaplan, Louisiana, in June of 1989. M. Hebert is a hotelier and storyteller in the Cajun tradition.

66. Provided by the Albuquerque Public Library in response to a request for further information on a series of fragments related to the editors during their stay in New Mexico in 1987. The story was reported in a November, 1913, edition of the *Albuquerque Evening Herald* under the heading "Ghost of Old Spaniard Haunts Punta de Agua." The fragments are presented with lacunae filled in (comments in brackets) from our own research.

We offer two alternatives to details in the often-repeated story: In the newspaper account, the Spaniard is described as "wearing the uniform of a French soldier": we believe this to be the tabard-with-cross of *Three Musketeers* fame, a garment worn in

Spain as well as France, with the cross of Calatrava, a purely Spanish emblem in spite of the presence of the *fleur-de-lys*. The newspaper story has the Spaniard say, *"Siste, viator,"* (stop, visitor) in Latin, apparently a language the tourist who saw the ghost had learned in grammar school; we suggest, based on fragments that have come to us, that the true message was in antique Spanish of the 1600s—which the ghost would more likely speak, and which the tourist would probably not have known. The original sighting was by a Wilbur S. Saener, of Winonk, Illinois, and some interested parties speculate that the "figure" has not been seen since, only reported by persons who wished the legend to grow and enhance the folklore of the region.

67. Provided by the Albuquerque Public Library in response to inquiries into a story that had appeared in 1952 in the *Tucumcari American-Leader,* and based on fragments provided to the editors at the Old Route 66 Café in Tucumcari in 1987. The story is still told in the area, primarily because of its punchline ending. Some versions of the story put the amount of payroll as high as $100,000 and refer to the money as being in "gold notes." Other versions apparently mention strongboxes full of gold bars or coins. The spiritualist explanation for the haunting is that the riders, so intent on their treasure, eternally reenact the opening of the boxes and the mysterious disposition of the gold (or banknotes).

68. The Riordan House is northern Arizona's most famous dwelling and seems to house Flagstaff's most famous ghost. Many interested parties speculate that the ghost is that of Anna, who died of polio, tradition says, within the house. Research by Paul Sweitzer, of the *Flagstaff Sun* newspaper staff, indicated that Anna died in a nearby hospital founded by the Riordan family. Our informant, who worked at the Riordan House under her maiden name Margaret Ybarra, refers to the ghost as that of Caroline, Anna's mother, still moving about the mansion, continuing to care for it after her death. The former Srta. Ybarra told the editors this personal experience, which we have extracted from a longer conversation while visiting at the Riordan House, now a small state park, on December 31, 1990. The Riordan brothers made their fortune in lumber, and the magnificent log mansion is still under restoration as of this writing.

69. Retold from versions common in the area of Guerra and Agua Nueva, Texas, heard in 1986. The severed hand gripping the reins is a well-known European folk motif. The phantom at El Blanco Rancho is also often desribed as being female, with a hideously decomposed face, perhaps as an alternative *LLorona*-figure. Each version bears different, usually conflicting, details.

70. Retold from the local legendry as provided by a waitress in a German-American restaurant, The Gasthaus, on November 17, 1990. Cripple Creek has many mining-related ghost stories, but they belong to a different collection.

71. Collected prior to January 1, 1989, from a family from Wichita, Kansas, who told the story solely for amusement and as "local Kansas lore," using the name "The Wraith of White Woman Creek."

72. Learned from Homer H. Young, Ph.D., in the summer of 1962. Dr. Young was a graduate of Austin College in Sherman, Texas, and played football in the 1920s when some players shaved their heads under their leather helmets. Rival Trinity University was founded in 1869 in Tehuacana, Texas, and moved in 1902 to Waxahachie and to San Antonio in 1942. Chief Tawakoni was a real person, but much information about him is legendary. The Wichita Indians were moved from the Canadian River area of Oklahoma to the Wichita Indian Reservation in 1859.

73. Provided by Arturo Jaramillo on December 30, 1989, at Rancho de Corrales Restaurant in Corrales, New Mexico. Sr. Jaramillo is one of the Torrez/Romero/Jaramillo family members who now own and manage the restaurant, formerly known as the Territorial House. The story of the Embertos' ghosts is one of the best-known ghost stories in Sandoval County, just as the restaurant is one of the best in the county.

74. The tale of the ghostly guardian on the Neches is retold by Texas folklorist J. Frank Dobie and a host of others. Versions vary, but interestingly enough, the quote of the man in the hole (sometimes called C—— and sometimes called Clawson) is always exact: "I have seen Hell and its horrors." Some have suggested it was a ruse, and the partner returned for the treasure; others prefer the ghostly—and ghastly—explanation and ending given here. Editor Richard Alan Young first heard this tale from his uncle Homer Harry Young, Ph.D., while spending the summer of 1962 in the Houston area. *See also the note for story number 10.*

75. There are several places in America known as Hell's Half Acre. The more legendary one is in Wyoming, along the Oregon Trail. Another is in Arkansas, and various versions of the explanation have come to the editors over the years, usually from hunters. The narrative first entered print when a Miss Clara Eno submitted a story to Alsop's classic story collection *Romantic Arkansas* in the 1920s.

76. This widely-known tale is told throughout New Mexico. One New Mexican told us this variant and mentioned the version found in B. A. Botkin's *A Treasury of American Folklore.* Our

version, collected in December, 1987, has details not in the Botkin variant and lacks some details therefrom.

77. This is a Hispanic story that some people say "ought not to be told." A grotesque variant on the "Golden Arm" theme, it is one of the oldest in the repertory of editor Richard Alan Young. It has been heard, among other places, at a gathering of college student members of Kappa Kappa Psi Fraternity in Tempe, Arizona, in August, 1968.

78. Collected from Tom Phillips, a former Harding College employee, on August 6, 1990. Mr. Phillips is a food service manager in his 30s who shares tales with the students at his college workstations.

79. Collected on June 25, 1990, from Sean Bishop of Altus, Oklahoma, telling about his true experiences in northern New Mexico in 1980. Mr. Bishop is a commercial pilot as of this printing. In the summers between years at the Air Force Academy, he worked as a ranger at Philmont Scout Camp in Cimarron, New Mexico, leading Scouts on camping and backpacking expeditions. While scary stories are stock-in-trade around Scout campfires, Mr. Bishop swears these are the truth. *(See also story number 16.)*

80. Collected from nationally-known storyteller and and petroglyph expert Teresa Pijoan de Van Etten in Placitas, New Mexico, on December 3l, 1989. Sra. Van Etten has published her own anthologies of native-American and Spanish-American stories *(see the note for story number 40)*. This and stories numbered 81 and 56 form a trilogy, which she told in sequence.

81. The second in the "El Cabezón Trilogy." See note 80 above.

82. Collected from George White, a member of the jury that convicted Odus Davidson, by Patricia Greeson, his granddaughter. Learned in childhood in the 1950s. Provided to the editors June 11, 1990.

83. Provided by Georgianna Greeson to the editors June 11, 1990. Mrs. Greeson was a resident of Arizona at the time of the events.

84. Provided by Fred and Vivian Hurlburt, storytellers from Golconda, Nevada, in January of 1991. Mrs. Hurlburt pointed out to these editors that Nevada has many ghost towns but few ghost stories. "Cousin Jack" refers to a Cornishman, and a *pastie* is a fried meat pie.

85. Collected in December, 1987, from one of the Acoma Indian women who serve as guides for tours of "Sky City," an Acoma pueblo in New Mexico. The 600-year-old pueblo sits atop a once impregnable mesa, and the ancestral home of the people is nearby

Enchanted Mesa, called Katzimo (spelled here phonetically) in the Keres language of Acoma.

86. This event happened in 1964 to Pat Echeté. She offered an alternate explanation: there was at that time a gas-well flare near the site, but its flame and glow were yellow; she discounts this explanation. She relates that this was the most popular ghost story in that area (St. Charles Parish) in her youth. Collected June 11, 1990.

87. Collected from Kathryn Cavert on June 11, 1990, at a large ghost-story telling session. Mrs. Cavert was a California resident at the time of the events of the story.

88. Learned from Dolan Ellis, the official balladier of the State of Arizona, in Scottsdale, Arizona, in December, 1985. Mr. Ellis has also written and published a song by the title of "Lady of the Ledge," and saw the lady while at Old Oraibi years ago.

89. Learned prior to January 1, 1989, by the editors while touring the area of Victoria, Texas, in the winter of 1984.

90. Provided by Kathy Costa and the Library Storytellers of Santa Fe, New Mexico. Mrs. Costa is a librarian at Oliver LaFarge Branch Library. Mrs. Costa and her sister Mrs. Grathwol *(see note for story number 61)* told many stories for the editors seated around a warm fire in the *horno* fireplace at Mrs. Costa's home in Santa Fe, January 3, 1990.

91. Collected by Terry Bloodworth from Mike Jenkins and passed along to the editors in October, 1990. Both men have worked in entertainment in the Branson, Missouri, area for many years.

92. Provided by Fred and Vivian Hurlburt, storytellers from Golconda, Nevada, in January of 1991. Most Nevada ghost stories deal with mining, and most are centered around the Virginia City area.

93. Collected from Johnny Brewer from Grove, Oklahoma, in August, 1989.

94. Collected from Terryl Hébert in August, 1989. M. Hébert, a hotelier and Cajun storyteller, had learned it from his father, Frank Hébert during his childhood in Crowley, Louisiana.

95. Provided by two brothers living in Scottsdale, Arizona, who often camp in the Superstitions and are acquainted with the legends, lore, and humbug of the mountains. Working as muleskinners at Rawhide theme park in Scottsdale, they provided this story, which may be passing into and out of the print medium, to the editors in early January, 1985. They tell all lore of the Superstitions as the truth, even conflicting stories.

96. Collected from Tracy Gerlach, owner of Process One in Harrison, Arkansas, at a ghost storytelling session June 11, 1990. The print mentioned in the story is in the collection of the editors and is the inspiration for the artist's rendering on the cover of this collection. Thousands of questions come to mind when one looks at the print. The photo shows no signs of fakery; the lab at Process One is not equipped for photographic fakery. Could it be a prank by one of the hunters...black cloth draped over a tree? The narrative has all the "stuff of urban legend," third-hand narrative, casual details, limited—but tempting—evidence, the terrible fate of those who saw the apparition, and so on. Mr. Gerlach offered one last comment: "The guy said apparitions are often that tall."

97. Collected in 1977 from Eddie Smith of Ogden, Arkansas, in Little River County. The town of Fouke sits in the marshy area at the confluence of the Red and Sulphur Rivers in southwest Arkansas, in Miller County. The monster was seen between 1955 and 1975, and the movie "The Legend of Boggy Creek" relates most of the reported sightings in semi-documentary form. Some suggest the creature is real—not a hallucination or myth—but is nothing more than a full-grown chimpanzee that escaped from a circus truck or exotic–pet owner. As an example of the species' longevity, readers of the tabloids were surprised to learn from the June 5, 1990, *National Enquirer* that Cheetah of the Tarzan movies was alive and well at age 55. Cheetah was at that time as large as his owner-trainer Tony Gentry, who brought the chimp from Africa in the 30s. Gentry was 86 and devoted to his simian star, who outlived most of the human stars of the Tarzan and other jungle movies in which he appeared. While there have been no recent sightings of the Fouke Monster, it remains an Arkansas–Texas phenomenon of immense folk popularity. There are Fouke Monster jokes, Fouke Monster folksongs, and so on.

98. This story was learned in fragmentary form from a merchant in the market in Nogales, Sonora, across the border from Nogales, Arizona, January 1, 1988. There are many versions of the story, ranging from European to Southwestern. One excellent version, perhaps more complete than this one, is entitled "Doña Sebastiana" and appears in *Cuentos* by José Griego Maestas and Rudolfo Anaya, based on the stories collected by Juan B. Rael.

99. This folktale about Death being tricked was reconstructed from two summary/fragments collected in Arizona and New Mexico in 1984–1988. Ethnically, the informants were more "cowboy" than Hispanic, and elements of the Appalachian folktale "Mean John and the Devil" seem to have been interpolated, either by poor memory or conscious adaptation. The central character, Pedro de Urdemalas, is a classic folkhero in Spain, where Miguel de Cer-

vantes Saavedra wrote a play by that name in 1617. The name "Urdemalas" means "Wreaks Pranks" or "Trickster;" he is often compared to—and his name translated as—"Artful Dodger," after the character in Charles Dickens's *Oliver Twist*. A truer Hispanic version appears under the name "Pedro de Ordimalas" in *Cuentos* by José Griego y Maestas and Rudolfo Anaya, based on narratives originally collected by Juan B. Rael in New Mexico and Colorado in 1977. Our primary source was a conversation with native Arizonans while we were appearing at Rawhide, a theme park in Scottsdale.

100. Collected from Teresa Pijoan de Van Etten in Placitas, New Mexico, December 31, 1987. The story is Seneca in origin and is told now by many tribal groups. In the Tewa Indian language tradition, stories are usually told in the frost months when the snakes are in their dens. An exception is made for stories that involve only human characters and for stories about flight. Sra. de Van Etten, a renowned storyteller and petroglyph expert, grew up in the San Juan Pueblo north of Santa Fe. She is the author of *Ways of Indian Wisdom* and *Ways of Indian Magic,* published by Sunstone Press in Albuquerque, and *Spanish-American Folktales,* published by August House, as well as other books. The editors have heard numerous versions of the Flying Head story, which is a favorite among children. The Van Etten family have been the gracious hosts of three storytelling sessions around the fire in their home in Placitas on the *fin del año* (New Year's Eve) of 1987, 1988 and 1989. The eve of a new year represents a crack in time, between the years, and it is a time when spirits could walk and graves open: the perfect time for ghost stories. The inspiration for this collection comes largely from these storytelling sessions, and the editors wish to express their appreciation to the Van Ettens for their contributions to the collection.

101a. Many historians in Texas and New Mexico repeat variations on the story of the Blue Lady. Her existence was reported by Fr. Alonso de Benavides in his *Memorial,* written in 1630. Fr. Damián Manzanet wrote in 1690 of her previous appearances to the Caddo Indians (or Tejas Indians.] The young mystical authoress María de Jesús de Agreda, who wrote *The Mystic and Divine History of the Virgin, Mother of God* in 1627, claimed that she had experienced "out-of-body" visitations to New Mexico, making her a "living ghost" by the definition of many psychic researchers. Historian Charles E. Chapman identifies de Agreda as the Blue Lady, but other writers leave her a supernatural mystery. The editors have heard versions and fragments of this story in New Mexico and Texas. This version was collected from Anglos and Hispanos; for a Pueblo Indian version, see next story.

101b. Provided anonymously from a source in the Santo Domingo Pueblo. The Blue Lady is revered by Indians, Anglos and Hispanos. *See also the Anglo and Hispano version in version above.*

102. Collected from students at the University of Texas at El Paso during an intercollegiate meeting with members of Kappa Kappa Psi Fraternity from the University of Arkansas in 1966.

103. The Wolf Girl legend has circulated among men and boys for more than a century in Texas. The mere fascination of seeing a naked girl running wild was enough to make this a prime campfire story in the 1950s, when this editor first heard it. L. D. Bertillion says, in *Straight Texas,* edited by J. Frank Dobie and Mody C. Boatright, in 1937, (Texas Folklore Society, Number XIII) that wolves "strongly marked with human characteristics" have been seen by him personally in that area. This grotesque postscript resembles a Greek myth more than a Texas legend.

104. Retold from the account of a teen-aged girl named Winona, who preferred not to be identified further, at a storytelling session in the early 1980s. She was a Texas resident at the time of the events of the story, which she related as the truth. The events so closely resemble the East Texas Hairy Man storyline (see the Introduction) that folklorists would assume it is merely a variant thereof. It was told, however, as the "Gospel truth."

105. This fragment was learned in Texas, near Abilene, from a Boy Scout storytelling session in the 1950s. The White Steed is told about from Texas to Arizona in story, poem, and song, always without a plotline.

106a. and 106b. The story about the "witch" Sally Baker was learned by Ken Teutsch of Walker's Creek, Arkansas, in his boyhood; he provided the "myth" and the postscript true story of his family's "debunking" of the myth on July 2l, 1990. Mr. Teutsch believed the witch tale until he spoke with his father in the 1970s. As a writer in television and other media, Mr. Teutsch's poignant postscript gives remarkable insight into the process by which commonplace events may be expanded to legendary proportions through the medium of the oral scary story. Mr. Teutsch insisted that both the myth and his personal involvement be included consecutively to suggest that part of the folkloric process.

107. This Tewa story is told in Santa Clara and San Ildefonso Pueblos, and was provided by Teresa Pijoan de Van Etten in 1990, with changes being made in the story to remove its spiritual power without changing the events of the story. Mushboy was made at other times and had other adventures as well. Mushboy is a favorite with children, and this story was conveyed in English. We and the teller shared a laugh as the teller struggled to say

Medicine-Meal Mush Boy, a tongue twister in English but not in Tewa.

108. Provided by Teresa Pijoan de Van Etten, of Placitas, New Mexico, this Hopi story came from the Arizona Hopi Homeland through a marriage. While it is not a sacred story, which the editors of this collection would not be entitled to hear and share, this story does have small changes made by the storyteller to remove its spiritual power and make it a touching moral lesson that may be read by anyone. If there is any error in our recording of this story, it is through ignorance, not disrespect. The story was told as an example of "teaching stories," which instruct children in proper behavior. Some of them are also scary stories that children love to hear over and over. Native American spirit stories resemble European ghost stories in this respect.

109. Provided by Judy Pruitt, storyteller for Rawhide theme park in Scottsdale, Arizona. This ghost train is often confused with, or its legend merged with, another ghost train seen in the distance across burning desert sand: a mirage caused by wavering hot air and a distant dust-devil that resembles a smoking stack. Mrs. Pruitt told this legend around a campfire in the Old Mission Patio at Rawhide on New Year's, 1991.

110. Collected from Teresa Pijoan de Van Etten in Placitas, New Mexico, December 31, 1989.

111. Provided by Barbara Pijoan and Teresa Pijoan de Van Etten of Corrales and Placitas, New Mexico, respectively, in December, 1989.

112. Collected by Teresa Pijoan de Van Etten and passed along to the editors on December 31, 1989. The story is well-known in the area around Española.

113. There are dozens of versions of the Stampede Mesa story, with some sources saying the names of participants have been forgotten, others offering pseudonyms (like Jones) and still others claiming to know the actual names of one or more historical characters. In some versions the rustler (or nester, in some versions) is killed before the stampede, in others he is killed for revenge and left to rot after he causes the stampede. The editors have heard this story from numerous informants in Texas since the 1950s. Storms often cause stampedes, but cattle could also be stampeded by something as small as a rabbit jumping in front of a lead steer; often the stampede's cause remained a mystery. Semi-literate cowboys relied largely on experience and verbal memory, so lore passed on by other cowboys had great significance and could cause superstition: a ghostly explanation for an unexplained stampede made as much sense as any. On another note, the physical phenomenon of an image projected

on low clouds is rare but documented: it was first named The Spectre of the Brocken for its appearance on a specific peak in Switzerland. Light from a setting or rising sun is focused through a "lens" of warm air or cold air and a focused shadow of a man on the peak is cast on the clouds beyond him. This phenomenon could theoretically have occurred, even only once, at Stampede Mesa, and the lore that arose around it would endure indefinitely. The Stampede Mesa story has merged in this variant with the Riders in the Sky motif, made famous as the song "Ghost Riders in the Sky" by Gene Autry and, later, Johnny Cash, and epitomized, some say, by Frankie Lane's rendition.

114. Learned from Chinese-Americans from California prior to January 1, 1989. The corpse-walkers operated in the high mountains of China and Tibet, but legend has it that one or more also provided the grisly service to the families of Chinese who died mining high in the Sierra Nevada in California in the 1800s.

115. Collected by Teresa Pijoan de Van Etten from Charlotte Perry-Martínez, who was told the story by her neighbor; he had been the *hijo desobediente* and had gone to the dance in Placitas, New Mexico, decades before. Provided to the editors in December of 1989.

116. Collected from Father Regis at the Church of San Miguel, on the Old Santa Fe Trail in Santa Fe. The stories associated with the bell and told by the Christian Brothers to all visitors are considered ghostly in that they deal with the Holy Ghost and the intervention of supernatural powers into the natural world. This miracle story would not be considered a ghost story among Protestants or Northern Europeans, whose "ghost traditions" are so different from the Hispanic views on the subject. Collected January 4, 1990.

117. This story is retold from the collection work of Texas folklorist Peggy Shamburger Hendricks, as provided to the editors in November, 1989. This story used to be told to Mrs. Hendricks by her great-aunt Betty Shamburger Atwood of Tyler, Texas, who had in turn learned it in about 1900 from her family's nurse and cook, Aunt Hattie. Aunt Hattie was of mixed native American and Negro ancestry, and the story shows both heritages. While Aunt Hattie's words of almost a century ago have been filtered through retelling, the heart of the story is perfectly preserved in this excellent version. This story is known by many names and variants. In the Southeast, it is called "Barney McCabe" or "Wylie and His Sister." In the Southwest, it is called "Wham, Jam, Jenny-Mo-Wham" or other variants of the witch's chant.

118. Retold from a California hunter, who provided the narrative in response to a hunting "tall tale" from the Ozarks, prior to January

1, 1989. The white male in his 50s told the story as the truth although he did not actually say if he had seen the booger deer personally.

119. Collected from Terry Bloodworth, a Judsonia, Arkansas, native, on October 25th, 1990, in Stoneridge, Missouri. The name "Creature-in-the-Hole" was used to describe this river monster; that name has been applied to numerous other creatures and sites in Arkansas and Missouri.

120. Collected from "Pa" Paddy by Terry Bloodworth in the 1960s and passed along to the editors October 25, 1990. Mr. Paddy firmly believed the story, according to Mr. Bloodworth; the "changing man" or "shape changer" is a character in the folklore of Gypsies, American Indians, Ozark hillbillies, and others.

121. Provided by Debbie McGown Steinmetz of West Jordan, Utah, January 21, 1991. The Three Nephites have appeared singularly or as a trio since the inception of the Church of Jesus Christ of Latter Day Saints. The way in which the Nephite narratives seem to blend with the tradition of the urban legend of the "Vanishing Hitchhiker" is a phenomenon that fascinates folklorists. The act of vanishing immediately after doing a good deed or making a prediction has been a practice attributed to the Nephites since their first appearances.

122. The Dineh (Navajo) hero Killer-of-the-Alien-Gods had many, many adventures; his adventure with He-Who-Kicks-People-Down-Cliffs is fairly well-known in the Southwest due to its mention in a Tony Hillerman novel.

Several Indian and non-Indian Southwesterners have given us fragments of this story, but for a telling close to the Dineh original, we have retold the event from *Navaho Legends* by Washington Matthews, *Memoires of the American Folk-Lore Society*, Volume V (New York, G. E. Stechert & Co., 1897). We have included one fragment from an informant: we were told that the story comes from the area of Navajo Mountain, Utah, and that the *anayei* (demon) lived on Gray Mesa in northern Arizona. The mountain the Dineh call Mount San Mateo is Mt. Taylor, New Mexico, and another explanation for the origin of El Cabezón is found in the story "The Devil's Neck" in this collection.

123. The legend of the White Riders is common in the Southwest, and has passed out of the oral tradition into print, and back into the oral tradition again. The story is sometimes recited as a poem or song, and sometimes told as a narrative. This version purports to be from the Drag-Eight Ranch, and was provided to the editors by an Arizona retiree, complete with obligatory turquoise-set string tie, at a story-telling session at Rawhide theme park in

Scottsdale, Arizona, on New Year's Day, 1991. The gentleman was an Anglo, in his seventies, who told the story as the gospel truth.

124. Collected from Bob Coody on December 31, 1990. Mr. Coody told this personal commentary with a nostalgic smile. The editors have extracted from a longer conversation this narrative about the spirits in the physical anthropology collection. It must be noted that the Museum of Northern Arizona treats the collection with the proper respect and works closely with the Hopi people, whose ancestors the collection represents. Mr. Coody is a librarian at the Northern Arizona University Special Collections Library in Flagstaff.

125. The Monster of the Mogollón Rim is a well-known Scout story used to frighten tenderfeet around the campfire. The editors first encountered a variant of this story with Scouts in New Mexico; an argument could be made that all the monster-in-the-night-that-gets-bad-Scouts stories are variants on a single theme. Most camps have a "patron spook" whose lore grows with each generation of Scouts and is perpetuated reverently in the most ancient of human rituals, storytelling around the campfire.

   The monster may be an Anglo version of the Navajo "Skinwalker," who challenges young men to prove their bravery against him.

126. A certain number of the stories in this collection are composites, reconstructed from fragments or constructed from variants wherein the lacunae in one version are filled by details from another, and vice-versa. These stories were collected prior to January 1, 1990, some as long ago as thirty years, and are not substantiated by collection notes. They are now elements of the repertory of Richard and Judy Dockrey Young, collected from the oral tradition, as told to them by the hundreds of kind informants and contributors they have met through the years. This is one such story.

127. Collected from Homer H. Young, Ph.D., who as a teen-ager was the perpetrator of the knocking on the carwall. He told the story with great amusement in the 1950s and 1960s; the events took place in the 1920s. The story was told as the truth.

128. Collected in fragments from Yoichi Aoki in 1973, with contributions by Marilyn Aoki in 1984 and Suzette Raney in 1990. Called "Yotsuya Kaidan," ("The Ghost Story from Yotsuya", or "It Happened in Yotsuya") this story has so many variants that some bear no resemblance to others, beyond the name itself. This is the favorite ghost story of the Nisei people of California.

129. From the repertory of Judy Dockrey Young. *See the note for story number 126.*

130. Provided by Dennis and Judy Pruitt, of Phoenix, Arizona, in January of 1991. Mrs. Pruitt is the storyteller at Rawhide theme park in Scottsdale. The person to whom the story happened wrote it down and used the title "Hand of Time." Certain words have been omitted that might have identified the family involved.

131. Collected in Fort Hays, Kansas, on November 26, 1990, at McDonald's over breakfast, from an elderly white lady who told it as the truth. A lifelong resident of Fort Hays, she spoke reverently of Elizabeth, Fort Hays's fairly famous ghost.

132. "La Llorona" from "La Llorona in Yuma" published in *Southwest Folklore*, Volume V Number 1, Winter 1981. Collected by Belinda F. Lopez in Yuma, Arizona, in 1981 from "Informant A.D., 37, male, half Mexican–American and half white [meaning Anglo]," and included in the above-named article written by Arizona folklorist Keith Cunningham. Reprinted by permission of the editor. This story is notable because of the motif of the Spanish man "legally" marrying a Spanish woman to promote his career and improve his social position. The collector, Srta. Lopez, pointed out that this version is not the most common one. Although collected in Yuma, Informant A.D. had first learned the story in neighboring Algodones, in Mexico, and the story would also be well-known in Imperial County, California.

133. Texas folklorist J. Frank Dobie gives a history of Jean Laffite in *Coronado's Children*. The pirate was born in France or Spain—stories vary—and perhaps at St. Malo or Orduña; either birthplace would give him an exotic lineage, Breton or Basque respectively. On existing historical documents, he spelled his name "Laffite," the spelling this collection employs. As a blacksmith shopowner on Bourbon Street in New Orleans, he took up with privateers on Barataria Island and became their entrepeneur/leader. Operating with letters of marque entitling them to raid the ships of one nation in behalf of a warring nation, the privateers raided indiscriminately and sold the goods and slaves in New Orleans.

When the War of 1812 broke out, the British offered Laffite a commission to attack New Orleans; instead he reported the plot to the Americans. At first Laffite was rebuffed, but when the battle of New Orleans came about, Andrew Jackson accepted Laffite's service in manning two artillery batteries. President Madison pardoned the "banditti" that fought for the U.S. in the battle. In 1816, Laffite moved his headquarters to Galveston Island, near present-day Houston. When his men began to prey on American ships, the Navy surrounded his enclave and ordered him out in 1820. Dobie suggests that Laffite died in Yucatán in 1826. Others claim he died in a battle with a British merchantman or was lost at sea in a storm. Like much of Laffite's life, his death was a mystery.

Laffite's headquarters, called the Maison Rouge, was real, and at least some of the treasure stories must be true also. This story came to the editors from many conflicting sources before 1989.

134. There are several theories about the origin of the name "Petit Jean." He may have been a short Frenchman killed by Indians, or "he" may have been the lady of the local legend. The people around Morrilton tell this version, with its lovely ghost. The editors have heard many versions of this legend before 1989.

135. Collected in New Orleans from an anonymous informant in November, 1984. The historic Marie Laveau died in 1881; her death was reported in the New Orleans newspapers. The second Marie must have been her daughter and a perfect filial image of her. The actual grave was originally unmarked, but its location is pinpointed by voodoo tradition. Since voodoo is a religion, practitioners are naturally skeptical of outsiders recording their traditions.

136. Collected from a young Hispana receptionist at the Kit Carson House Museum on January 4, 1990.

137. Retold from an account by a New Mexico listener at a storytelling event in December, 1989. When the editors asked the curator of the Bent House Museum if the story were true, he smiled and answered only, "You'll hear all kinds of stories about this place."

138. Provided by L. E. Gay of Santa Fe in June of 1990. Mr. Gay is a rare–book dealer and knowledgeable of Santa Fe and New Mexico lore.

139. Learned from Texas visitors to Silver Dollar City prior to January 1, 1989.

140. Collected in June of 1989 from Louis Darby of Opelousas, Louisiana. M. Darby is a Cajun fiddle-player and sometime storyteller.

141. Collected from Roger Knight from St. Louis, Missouri, in July of 1989. Mr. Knight in his 20s once worked at the Lunt Mansion as a server.

142. Provided by a librarian at Harwood Library in Taos, New Mexico, the night of January 4, 1990. She declined to be identified. Mabel Dodge Luján and Tony Luján were mavens of Taos artistic society for years; they were beloved and controversial. Other fragmentary tales of falling statues and moving furniture have also been heard by these editors, but this short tale is the most substantial we have received.

For further study...

For storytellers and story researchers who wish to pursue further study of ghost and supernatural narratives from the American Southwest, we recommend the following books and sources:

❖ *Researcher's Guide (to Archives and Regional History Sources)*, edited by John C. Larsen, Library Professional Publications, The Shoe String Press, Inc., Hamden, Connecticut, 1988. See especially the articles "Oral Histories" by Willa K. Baum and Bonnie Hardwick, and "The Ethics of Archival Research" by Floyd M. Shumway. (ISBN 0-208-02144-2)

❖ *Directory of Oral History Collections*, by Allen Smith, Oryx Press, Phoenix, Arizona, 1988. See especially the entries under the headings "Folk Medicine Archive," "Folklore/Folklife," and "Folklore Archive," page 108. (ISBN 0-89774-322-9)

❖ *Directory of Archives and Manuscript Repositories in the United States (Second Edition: National Historical Publications and Records Commission)*, Oryx Press, Phoenix, Arizona, 1988. See especially the entries under the heading "Folklore," page 788.

The best source of folklore material is the "folks themselves." By going to the Southwest, or by corresponding with individuals living or reared in the Southwest, a storyteller or story researcher can best obtain folk narratives. If such an excursion or such communication is not feasible, here are suggested publishing houses and resource providers for story materials in print:

❖ August House Publishers, Post Office Box 3223, Little Rock, Arkansas 72203, telephone 1/800/284-8784. In addition to this anthology, August House publishes other folklore and stories collected or edited for reading, research, and telling. Write or call for a catalog.

❖ The National Association for the Preservation and Perpetuation of Storytelling (NAPPS), Post Office Box 309, Jonesborough, Tennessee 37659. Write for their current "Storytelling Catalog" or purchase their current *National Directory of Storytelling*. The *Directory* lists storytellers, storytelling organizations, newsletters, resources, festivals, conferences, and centers for storytelling.

Index of stories by chapter, showing states of origin

Index of stories by states of origin